ISLAND HOPPING

THE ESCAPE SERIES

ANN OMASTA

FREE NOVELLA!

Escape into the enchanting Hawaiian Islands by reading this heartwarming tale of friendship, love, and triumph after heartbreak.

Free when you join Ann Omasta's VIP reader group. We value your privacy. Just tell us where to send your free novella.

Visit annomasta.com for details.

I'm not overly surprised when I look out the window and see the naked, wrinkled, and saggy white butt pointed in my direction. Knowing this is just the woman's latest antic to try to get under my skin, I refuse to allow it to bother me.

After unlocking and raising my living room window, I yell outside through the screen, "Good morning, Baggy!"

Standing up to her full four feet, eight inches of height, with her pants still around her ankles, the spry little old lady turns around to glare at me. She's obviously disappointed that her prank didn't upset me.

Shaking my head, I decide the least I can do is play along with her ornery game. "That's a good one. You really got me this time, Baggy!"

At this the older woman beams and yanks her pants back up. Raising her fist in the air like she has just won a race, she toddles back down the road towards her house, without giving me another glance. Hopefully, that means she is done badgering me, at least for the rest of the day.

She has been trying for months to punish me for hurting her granddaughter, Roxy. I can't even get mad at the old lady's crazy shenanigans because I deserve whatever she dishes out in my direction.

Roxy is my best friend. *Or was.* We'd been best friends since our first day of preschool. The fact that I stole her fiancé, Gary, the night before her planned wedding to him still doesn't compute... even in my own mind. It is so far removed from everything I stand for. It's like I threw the whole 'sisters before misters' thing out the window for that brief moment in time. I can't believe I let that loser kiss me after their rehearsal dinner.

That ill-advised kiss set off a whirlwind of events, including Gary texting Roxy on the actual day of their planned nuptials to tell her the wedding was cancelled because he and I were in love.

The fact that he *texted* her with this information should have been a major clue to both of us that Gary was not a great catch. Telling her that he and I were in love because I made the mistake of letting him kiss me once is such a wildly preposterous leap that I almost wonder if the man is delusional.

He obviously was looking for any excuse to get out of marrying Roxy, but I wish with all my heart that I hadn't allowed myself to become his escape route.

The devastating turn of events actually worked

out for the best for Roxy. She met the man of her dreams, which is obviously not Gary, and is now madly in love with the hunk from Hawaii. This positive outcome doesn't negate the fact that my betrayal was wrong. I would love to go back to that night and make it right. That's obviously not a possibility, so I'm focusing on doing everything in my power to make it up to Roxy and gracefully accepting whatever punishments her sister, Ruthie, and grandmother, Baggy, deem appropriate.

Roxy has, for the most part, forgiven me for the transgression. We'll probably never be as close as we once were, but she is taking the high road and working to move past the giant rift I created between us.

Ruthie and Baggy, however, are showing no signs of ever forgiving, forgetting, or moving on. Their persistent fury with me hurts a great deal because the two of them had always been like my adopted family.

Roxy and I were so close growing up, that I spent almost more time at the Rose household than I did my own. I had always considered Ruthie to be my pesky kid sister, since I didn't have any siblings of my own. Although we teased and picked on her, I loved her as fiercely and unconditionally as if she were my sister by blood.

Baggy was in a category of her own. As a toddler, Roxy's childish version of 'bad grandma' had come out of her tiny mouth sounding like Baggy. The moniker was so appropriate that it had stuck. Everyone called her Baggy, not just family. In fact, I have no idea what her given name is. She's simply Baggy, and it suits her to a tee.

My maternal grandmother passed away at an early age. Since my father bailed on my mother before I was born, I don't know my paternal grandparents at all. Baggy stepped in from the time I was about five to brilliantly and unconventionally fill that vital role in my life. Although she is often wildly inappropriate and outrageous, I love her with all my heart. It devastates me that she is so angry with me, even though I deserve it.

As I slice a banana for my oatmeal, I sigh and smile as I think about all the crazy things Baggy has done over the years. Her daughter, Caroline, Roxy and Ruthie's stuffy mother, is constantly yelling at Baggy to behave, as if the younger woman is the parent.

Once my teapot whistles, I pour the hot water into my oatmeal bowl and into my pre-warmed tea mug. Dunking the orange pekoe teabag in the hot water, I realize that tea is such a priority in my life because of Baggy. Whenever any of us girls were upset about something, she was always there with a warm mug of tea and a soft, reassuring hug.

I can feel the tears glistening in my eyes as I realize how much I miss having her sometimes bonkers, always soothing presence in my life. One stupid kiss had lost me a best friend, a sister, and a grandmother. Not to mention the fact that I am now a social pariah in our small town.

The Rose family is beloved by all, and I have managed to alienate them. Until it was gone, I didn't realize how much of my social standing came from being accepted as an unofficial member of their family.

Biting my lip as I rinse the blueberries for my hot cereal, I try for the thousandth time to think of a way to make it up to them. Roxy claims to have forgiven me, but I know she will never forget what I did. Our relationship will likely never get back to what it was before that life-ruining kiss. Besides, she lives in Hawaii now, so it's not like we can hang out on a daily basis.

Ruthie and Baggy view my betrayal of Roxy as a personal affront. They are showing no signs of ever getting over it, and I can't say that I blame them. I wouldn't be able to forgive someone for hurting my sweet, caring, and wonderful friend, either. In fact, I haven't forgiven myself, so why should I expect them to do so?

I eat my breakfast without really tasting it. The morning news program is on, but I can't focus on it. I'm such a fixer at work, it boggles my mind that I can't carry that talent over into my personal life and make things right with my three favorite ladies (other than my own mother, of course).

Speaking of my mom, I know she is ashamed of my transgression. She hasn't ever called me out on it, but I can tell that she is disappointed. Being seen with me in public has made her an outcast in town, too, and for that, I am truly sorry. I don't know what to do to make it up to her, other than to try to earn the forgiveness of Roxy's family.

Roxy and Ruthie's parents are civil whenever we bump into each other, but they are even more standoffish than they used to be. They never have been my biggest fans, but they permitted me to be absorbed into the folds of their family as an honored guest. I'm sure they feel betrayed by my mistake too.

The knock at my front door startles me out of my rumination as I rinse out my empty bowl and mug. After drying off my hands with the red and white kitchen towel that reads, *Kiss the Cook*, which Ruthie gave me as a housewarming gift when I bought this condo a few years ago, I head to answer it.

Already knowing who is probably on the other side and hoping to curb any more of her pranks for the day, I yell, "I have to finish getting ready for work, Baggy."

Wondering if she had simply 'ding-donged and dashed,' or if she had left me an unpleasant surprise, like a bag of flaming dog poop, I fling the door open.

"Oh!" I yell out in surprise at the slick-looking businessman on the other side of the door. Suddenly, I wish that I could be better about being a little more stringent with security, like peering through the peephole before opening my door to strangers.

"Expecting a batty old woman?" The man's exaggerated smile reveals an abundance of big, white teeth. It reminds me of a cartoon shark.

I am perplexed by how he knows Baggy and a little affronted by what he has called her. His description is perfectly accurate, but my hackles are raised nonetheless.

Feeling annoyed by his obvious arrogance, I snap, "I don't have time for uninvited guests. Whatever you're selling, I don't want."

My strong, negative reaction to this man surprises me, but I'm in too far to back down now. With a brisk nod, I soften my previous sentiment by adding, "Good day."

When I try to slam the door shut, he sticks his shiny leather, expensive-looking shoe in the opening to keep the door from fully closing.

I gape at him, stunned by his audacity. As he reaches into his pocket, my first thought is that he might be reaching for a weapon, so I am immediately relieved when he pulls out a business card.

He shoves the card through the opening his foot is demanding. I decide to accept it in the hope that he will then leave.

Glancing down at the thick card stock, I am surprised to see only one line of embossed lettering… 'T.J. Stone, Producer.'

2

*T*he name sounds familiar. I know that I
have heard it somewhere before, but I
can't quite put my finger on exactly who T.J.
Stone is.

As I stare at the card and try to discern how I
know this uninvited guest, I evidently ease up my
pressure on the door. The smooth producer uses
my distraction to slide his way through my front
door. When I look up, he is standing in my
entryway.

"Figure it out yet?" His eyes are practically
dancing, alight with the knowledge that he has the
upper hand.

I start to shake my head, but something about
his gleeful expression jogs my memory. I've seen
that look before. It is the same expression he wore
when he ruined several people's lives by sharing
their most-guarded secrets on live streaming
television.

"You're the crocodile from *Cruising for Love*." I

say the words flatly, already feeling confident that I have pinpointed exactly who he is.

T.J. tips his head back and laughs at that. It's obvious that his unflattering nickname doesn't bother him in the slightest. Once his laughter subsides, he says, "That's Ruthie's pet name for me. I'm surprised she shared that with you. I was under the impression that the two of you don't get along."

Ruthie hadn't shared that detail or anything else with me in a very long time. I had overheard her talking about him at a restaurant, but I am not willing to admit that to the man who tried to ruin her life on reality television. He would view our tiff as a juicy tidbit to use against her the next time he manages to lure her onto one of his shows.

Refusing to play his game, I lift my chin and say, "We get along just fine. Now, if you'll excuse me, I need to finish getting ready for work."

Shaking his head, he makes 'tsk' sounds as if he is disappointed in me. "I know that Ruthie hates you, and I know why."

I hate it that this jerk seems to know as much about my life as I do, but I refuse to be a pawn that he can later twist around to use against Ruthie. Inserting determination in my voice, I tell him, "It's time for you to go."

His facial expression morphs into one of sympathy. Ignoring my request that he leave, he says, "It must be so tough being hated by your closest friends, over one brief instant of bad judgment."

I give him a brisk nod and move my hand to usher him back out my open front door.

"I'd like to help you win them back, Lizzie."

His words sound sincere. My desperation to make amends with Roxy, Ruthie, and Baggy makes me long to believe him, but I know that he is not to be trusted.

Seeming to sense my wavering conviction, the croc goes in for the kill. "The best way to earn back their trust and affection would be for you to join us for Ruthie's live-streamed wedding. My guess is that there will be numerous things go wrong. Your particular skills will come in handy. If you save her special day, they'll have no choice except to forgive you."

Even though I know he is likely setting me up in a trap, it is tempting to accept his offer. I will do about anything to make amends with Ruthie. Voicing my top concern, I say, "They don't want me to come to the wedding. I'll end up making things worse between us if I show up uninvited."

"Perhaps," T.J. shrugs his shoulders before adding, "But Ruthie tends to be a little scatter-brained and accident-prone. I'd hate for her wedding, that the whole world is watching via the internet, to become a complete fiasco."

I see right through his innocent façade. Narrowing my eyes, I accuse him, "You're planning to set her up to fail."

"Ruthie has a tendency to do plenty of that on her own, without any of my help."

It isn't lost on me that he has managed to avoid addressing my allegation. I'm fairly certain that he has some evil plans to sabotage her big day. His goal is to have great ratings for his show. A perfect, gorgeous wedding won't bring nearly as many views and sponsors as a completely disastrous one.

Confirming my suspicions without actually uttering the words, the producer adds, "If you're there to fix issues as they arise, Ruthie will have a lovely wedding. If you're not in attendance, well…" He shrugs his shoulders and lets the implied threat dangle in the air.

I am at a loss for what to do. I know that Ruthie does not want me at her wedding. Her family will not welcome me with open arms. The last thing I want is to make them hate me more by showing up uninvited and unwanted.

On the other hand, I know that the crocodile is planning to wreak havoc on her wedding. If I'm there, I can help avert any crises and keep things running smoothly. Saving the younger Rose sister's wedding might help make up for ruining the older sister's big day, right?

I glare at him as I consider my options. It's obvious by his confidence in my skills that he knows what I do for a living. Being an Executive Assistant to the CEO of a multinational corporation means that I am adept at taking care of any problems that are thrown my way. From the tiny details, like picking the perfect tie for an event, to huge strategic decisions, I am the right-hand woman. Without me taking care of everything, so many balls would get dropped the company might never recover.

The show producers have been advertising the upcoming wedding for weeks. I know that it is scheduled to occur on some exotic, tropical island.

Inserting firmness into my voice, I say, "I can't leave my job."

Waving off my concerns, he says, "You've earned plenty of time off. Take it. They'll have to figure out a way to survive without you for a bit." He narrows his gaze at me, like a lion honing in on its prey. "Besides, Ruthie needs you."

And there it is. My job is important to me, but Ruthie is my chosen family. If there is a way for me to save the most monumental day of her life, then I need to do it. Accepting my fate, I nod and say, "If I rush, I can make the necessary arrangements for me to be off work for the wedding in two weeks."

Turning to head back outside, T.J. says over his shoulder, "We leave in twenty-four hours."

3

*A*s I had suspected, my boss, Dave, freaks out over my impending time off, but I don't leave him any other choice. I have saved his butt more times than I can count, so he owes me.

With true fear in his eyes, he asks, "What am I going to do without you?"

I know his question is sincere. I earned his trust not long after my arrival at the company as a temporary receptionist. He accidentally shared a naughty appointment from his calendar with the entire company. Rather than tell their boss about the faux pas, the employees snickered behind his back. I summoned all of my courage and emailed him about it. He immediately called me to his office. I thought for sure that I was going to be fired, but instead, he asked me to adjust the settings on his account to be private. He promoted me on the spot, and he has trusted me implicitly since that fateful day.

Inserting more confidence than I feel into my voice, I reassure him. "It will be fine. We have three Executive Assistants from the other C-level officers filling in during my absence. They can adeptly handle anything you throw their way."

"But they aren't you," he pouts.

I'm touched that he feels so strongly about my value as an employee, but I am unwilling to back down. "I'll be back as soon as I can."

"Many people mistakenly think that you're 'just a secretary,' but we both know that you're the one who gets things done around here. You run this office. Three people aren't enough to replace you."

Tears sting my eyes at his high praise, but I refuse to allow them to fall. With a brisk "Good-bye," I leave, before he can try to bribe me into staying. Ruthie needs me, and I intend to be there for her––even if she doesn't want me.

"What in the ever-lovin' hell of tarnation is she doing here?" Baggy asks the outraged question as soon as I join them in the airport's waiting area. I'm still feeling giddy from getting to use my passport that I've had for ages, but hadn't ever actually needed. Her words put a slight damper on my mood.

Ruthie looks like she has just been slapped as she bugs her eyes out in my direction. "I… I don't know."

Trying to look more confident than I feel, I smile and say, "I wouldn't miss your wedding for the world."

Ruthie is shaking her head as if she can't quite believe her eyes. "But you aren't invited. You can't come."

She turns to look at her fiancé, parents, and finally Baggy for support. Evidently finding the reassurance she needs in her grandmother's fired-up gaze, she turns to the older woman and says, "She *can't* come."

"Damn-tootin' right, she can't come." Baggy weighs in. Turning her rheumy eyes towards me, she adds, "We don't abide by traitors in our midst."

It is Ruthie's quiet father who sticks up for me. "Lizzie has been a part of this family for a long time. Isn't it time we forgive her?"

I try to show him with my gaze and a half-smile how much I appreciate him siding with me.

"Forgive her?!?" Baggy sounds truly affronted by the mere idea of it. "We don't do that." She waves her bent pointer finger back and forth to accentuate her words.

Clasping her fiancé's hand in a possessive manner, Ruthie glares at me. "She's probably here to try to steal Andrew away from me and ruin our wedding day."

"That could never happen," Andrew leans in and reassures her before adding to the larger group, "Maybe we should give her the benefit of the doubt. It took a lot of courage for her to come here."

We grew up in the same town, but I've only ever heard Andrew speak on television. I already like his calm, kind, and thoughtful demeanor. He seems to be the exact opposite of impulsive,

17

ANN OMASTA

flighty, and bubbly Ruthie. They must be a classic case of opposites attracting.

Striking while the tide of opinion seems to be shifting in my favor, I say, "I'm here to help. My guess is that there will be some snafus with the wedding planning and ceremony. I'll be in the background to step in and assist in making sure things run smoothly." As an afterthought, I add, "No matter what trials that crocodile producer tries to throw at us."

I can see that my words have startled Ruthie. Turning to Andrew, she asks, "You don't think T.J. would try to ruin our big day, do you?"

"I wouldn't put it past him," Andrew weighs in.

Baggy has her eyes narrowed in my direction. Lifting her gnarled finger to point at me, she asks, "How do we know she isn't a plant sent by him to ruin everything?"

Deciding I better address it directly, I reveal, "T.J. is the one who asked me to come." Someone gulps in air at that news, so I quickly add, "But I am only here to help and be a part of Ruthie's big day. I want it to go perfectly, and I won't be a part of anything that risks marring her dream wedding day."

I hope the sincerity of my words rings through in my tone. My gaze travels to each of them as I silently plead with them to let me join in the festivities to come.

Seeming to shift her opinion a tiny bit, Ruthie asks me, "Are you just here to try to become famous?"

I practically snort at that. "Umm, no. You can

have the spotlight. I am planning to stay off-camera as much as possible."

It seems like they are starting to waver in their steadfast hatred of me until Baggy squints at me and yells, "I ain't buyin' this bucket of hogwash! She's up to something."

"Mother, stop it." Ruthie's mom, Caroline, chastises her own mother.

The older woman glares at me, like a rebellious teenager who is sulking and plotting her revenge for a perceived wrongdoing. I've never before been on Baggy's bad side, and I don't like how it feels one bit. I will do anything in my power to get back in her good graces.

Caroline continues, ignoring Baggy's pouting. "Lizzie made a mistake. She has admitted that and apologized for it. It's time for us ALL," she gives her mother a pointed look down her glasses before continuing, "to forgive her and move on."

I've never been so grateful for anyone's mercy in my entire life. If I thought Caroline wouldn't stiffen up with discomfort, I would give the tall, generally-aloof woman a bear hug. Instead, I quietly whisper the words "Thank you" in her direction.

All eyes are on Ruthie, awaiting her decision. She doesn't appear to want to forgive me, but her parents and Andrew obviously think she should.

"Fine," she finally huffs. Turning, she glares eye darts at me before adding, "You can come, but if I see any funny business, you are out of there."

"I'll behave," I promise, nodding and breathing a sigh of relief.

Evidently deciding to make the best of it, Baggy yells out, "Hot damn! Turks and Caicos, here we come!"

No one bothers to correct her that we are heading to Antigua.

4

I wonder how much of what has just transpired will end up on the pre-wedding show. Cameramen are scattered throughout the waiting area recording every moment of our interaction.

Although I can't imagine ever getting used to having cameras shoved in my face, the others seem to not even notice their presence.

Feeling like the odd man out, I turn to the group at large. "I thought at the end of the last season, it was announced that Ruthie and Andrew's nuptials would be aired live from Vegas. Why are we heading to the Caribbean?"

"I'm not having a cheesy Vegas wedding," Ruthie snaps in my direction. After her eyes dart to the cameras, she softens her answer. "I mean, I've always dreamed of a picturesque beach-side wedding, and the show's producers are generously making all of my dreams come true."

I feel like rolling my eyes as she bats her lashes at the camera across from her. It is obvious that she is trying to make sure they don't get any clips they can use to make her look like a spoiled diva. Last year's shows made it clear that they can twist her words around to make her seem like a total brat. While Ruthie can be a bit self-centered, she is also fiercely loyal and caring. I hope they show those sides of her on this new show.

Ignoring her preening for the camera, I ask, "What is the new show called? I assume it's not *Cruising for Love*, since we won't be on a cruise ship." My voice squeaks when I ask, "Right?" The thought of spending a week heaving with seasickness over the side of a luxury liner does not sound in the slightest bit appealing, but I will do it, if it means I get to make up with Roxy's family.

Andrew answers me. "No cruise ships this time. The show is called *Dream Wedding Extravaganza*. We were allowed to pick our ideal wedding location."

The 'Extravaganza' wording worries me. It generally has a positive connotation, but knowing how the last show went, I wonder if they might mean it in the spectacular blowout sense of the word.

Before long, they begin calling the boarding of our plane. The entire gang, including the cameramen, gets up to present their first-class tickets and pre-board. I glance down at my boarding pass for coach. My hope is that this is merely a result of my ticket being a last-minute purchase, and not an indicator of intentional slights to come.

Deciding that I don't deserve the 'star' treatment, I smile up at them and say that I'll catch up with them when we land. Andrew looks like he feels guilty about leaving me behind, but Ruthie whispers something in his ear, so he quickly turns and heads hand-in-hand to the gate with her.

Once I am finally permitted to board the plane, I struggle to fit my carry-on through the narrow aisle. The mimosas are obviously free-flowing in first class. Baggy lifts hers up in my direction and proclaims this to already be the "best flight ever."

I smile at her and head to the back of the plane. My seat is on the aisle, adjacent to the restrooms in the aft of the aircraft. Either mine was the very last ticket available on this flight, or someone from the show has it out for me already.

Trying to make the best of it, I put on my neck pillow and try to doze off. The upright position of my seat makes that difficult, but I evidently manage because I wake up with drool dribbling down my chin when the Captain makes the announcement that we should prepare for landing. I lean around my seatmate to look out the small window as we land and am delighted to see the pink airport. *Anyplace with a pink airport has to be fun, right?*

Once we deplane and claim our luggage, a chauffeur indicates that he will take us to the resort. He does a quick head count, then recounts. Furrowing his brow, he says, "I only have room for eight passengers."

I glance around at Ruthie, Andrew, Ruthie's parents, Baggy, and the three cameramen. They are all looking back at me. "Oh… I'll catch a cab or something and meet you there."

Even though I had thought they might insist on squeezing in to make room or having someone stay back with me, they quickly agree and set off without me. I struggle with my luggage and head outside to try to find a ride.

The sun is shining brightly and the heat makes my skin feel hot to the touch. My hair is sticking to my face as I blow my bangs up and try to cool off a little. I sigh with relief when I am easily able to flag down a cabbie. Once inside, we careen off in what I hope is the direction of our hotel.

"Air conditioner?" I ask the driver, silently praying that he will turn it on and help me cool down.

"No," he responds briskly before motioning that I can roll down my windows. I do so, but am disappointed that it only creates a hot breeze that does nothing to help me cool down.

When we finally pull into the resort, I glance up at my reflection in the rearview mirror. Not only am I a sweaty mess, but now I have also added windblown into the mix. Silently deciding that I need to avoid the camera crew until I can get cleaned up, I curse out loud when I see a cameraman waiting outside to shoot my arrival.

Reminding myself that this isn't about me, I put on a bright smile and emerge from the cab. After getting my luggage and paying the driver, I smile at the camera as I walk by. Deciding self-effacing is probably my best bet at this point, I say, "Guess I'm the only one who traveled through a hurricane on my way here, huh?"

The cameraman ignores me, and I suddenly remember that I'm not supposed to interact directly with them. "Great start," I mumble, chiding myself as I go to check into my room.

5

I don't know why I'm surprised when the front desk clerk gives me a blank stare. I have her check under my name, Ruthie's, T.J.'s, the show, and everything else I can think of.

"Look, lady, we don't have a reservation for you, and we are booked to capacity."

Scanning the room, I look for anyone related to the show, who might be able to clear this up. The only person I recognize in the lobby is the cameraman standing just behind me. I turn to him and plead, "Can you please tell them that I'm part of the show, or let me know where I can find someone who can?"

He silently stares at me, but keeps the camera rolling. Annoyed, I snap, "You're about as helpful as a statue."

The man filming me has no reaction whatso-ever. The woman behind the desk is done with me. "Ma'am, there are registered guests, *with* reservations, behind you in line that are waiting to check in. We need you to step aside."

Not seeing another option, I turn around to begin looking for T.J. Proving that I do occasionally have good luck, he appears as if I have summoned him.

"Oh, thank heavens." I rush towards him. He bugs his eyes out for a moment, until recognition dawns on his face. "Lizzie, you made it!" He air kisses my cheeks as I try not to cringe at his fake, over-the-top friendliness.

"I did." I nod before adding, "But the front desk is telling me that I don't have a room reservation."

T.J. furrows his brow and snaps his fingers. A clipboard-carrying assistant magically appears to see what he wants. I am horrified that he has snapped for her in this manner. He needs to take some lessons from my boss, Dave, on how to treat employees with respect.

The assistant doesn't seem to notice the inappropriate gesture as she joins us and efficiently asks what she can do to help.

"Check on Lizzie's reservation," T.J. barks at her. "The front desk is claiming they don't have a room for her."

It is obvious by the way her face immediately falls that the woman was supposed to have made my reservation, but failed to do so. She looks down and shuffles papers on her clipboard, clearly frazzled by having forgotten to take care of this detail.

I recognize her panicked expression and long to keep her from getting into any trouble. Smiling at T.J., I say, "I think I know what happened. It's a simple misunderstanding. Sorry to have bothered you."

At my reassurance, he nods and moves on. The woman with the clipboard breathes out a huge sigh of relief as he walks away before turning to present her hand to me. "Thank you so much! My name is Jamie. I owe you one."

She pumps my hand vigorously, which makes me smile at her. "I'm glad to hear you say that, Jamie, because it just so happens that I am in need of a bed to sleep in while we're here. Any chance I can bunk in your room?"

Even though we are strangers, I'm hoping that she'll feel guilty enough about flubbing my reservation that she'll let me join her.

From the way her face falls, I can tell my idea isn't going to work out. "I'd love to fix this, but I'm sharing a room with the other female members of the crew. We are maxed out."

"Do you have a fold-out sofa or rollaway bed I could use?" I try, but she's shaking her head.

"We already have people in both of those spots. The show goes all out with the budget for the cast and to make the wedding look good, but the people behind the scenes are packed in like sardines."

Just as I'm getting ready to nod my acceptance of that and try to come up with a more creative solution, a man interrupts us. "Couldn't help but overhear your predicament."

He looks like a typical surfer-dude type with long, lush sunkissed blonde hair, overly-tanned skin, and a laid-back, island wardrobe consisting of board shorts, a tee-shirt picturing an underwater scene, and flip flops. His eyes are ocean blue, but the skin around them has big white circles. It is obvious that he regularly wears sunglasses, but doesn't bother with sunscreen.

I can't imagine why he is butting into our private conversation, so I raise my eyebrows and give him a cool stare.

Ignoring my semi-rudeness, he offers, "I might be able to help you out."

He has my attention now, so I respond, "Oh, how so?"

"You can stay at my place," he offers, as if this is the answer to all of my prayers.

Frustrated with myself for getting my hopes up that this beach bum might be able to help me, I give him a weary look before saying, "I don't think so," and turning back to Jamie.

Unwilling to be deterred so easily, hang-ten man says, "No, really. I have employee accommodations that you can use. It's not as fancy or luxurious as the guest rooms, but it has a bed and a shower."

I can't believe this perfect stranger is trying to lure me into staying in his room. Giving him my best sarcastic sneer, I say, "Tempting, but no."

In the hopes of shutting him down and sending him to bother someone else, I angle my body away from him and speak to Jamie. "Maybe we can find a nearby hotel with vacancy?"

Her eyes light up that this might work, until surfer boy clicks his tongue and says, "Closest hotel to here is the Mandarin Bay, but they are full-up."

I'm fully annoyed that he didn't take my not-at-all subtle hints that we don't need or want his help. Keeping my voice crisp, I say, "We've got this. Thanks."

"Suit yourself," he says, holding up his hands as if to say he tried, "But there's a perfectly fine, empty room that's all yours, if you just say the word."

He is already turning to leave when I ask, "Empty?"

"Yeah, I sleep out on my boat." He turns back to face us, so I can see the moment comprehension dawns on his face. "Oh… You thought I was insinuating that you stay in the room *with* me? No wonder you were being so bitchy."

Although I know I have been less-than-friendly with him, I still cringe at being called out by a stranger as being bitchy. Not seeming to notice my scrunched face, he goes on. "That's crazy, though. I wouldn't sleep with you. I don't even know you."

The fact that this man is acting as if my conclusion that he was trying to get me into bed was preposterous infuriates me. "It's not *that* far-fetched," I defend my initial reaction.

Somehow this jerk has me defending my merits as a choice for a one-night stand. Jamie is watching our entire interaction unfold as if it is the most amusing thing she has seen all day.

Clueless to my irritation, the stranger extends his hand and says, "I'm Shay Sanders."

Not seeing another option, I shake his hand. "Lizzie." I probably sound overly curt, since I don't share my last name, but this man irks me.

"Have a last name, Lizzie?" He smiles and

reveals bright, white teeth. The grooming of his shaggy hair might not be a priority, but dental hygiene obviously is. I'm annoyed to see that he has an adorable dimple on one cheek.

I'm not sure why he feels the need to know my last name, but it seems too rude to refuse to answer. I give him another one-word response, hoping that he'll stop the chitchat and jump to the part where he gives me a room to stay in. "Lowe."

"Your parents enjoy alliteration too, huh?"

Having made a snap judgment about him, based on his looks, I am surprised that he knows the meaning of the word 'alliteration.' Rather than voicing my mistaken conclusion, I nod in answer to his question before verbally nudging him, "You mentioned a room?"

He seems a bit taken aback by my abruptness, but he doesn't call me out on it. "Oh, right… Follow me."

He takes my luggage and turns to leave. I'm touched at his chivalry, but still bug my eyes out at Jamie to let her know she needs to come with us. She's the one who got me into this lack of a room situation, so the least she can do is come and make sure Shay isn't a serial killer trying to lure me into his creepy lair.

The other woman doesn't even try to put up a fight about coming with us. We walk for what seems like miles. The resort is much bigger than I imagined, sprawling across several acres.

I feel the sweat dripping down my side as I trudge along behind Shay, which makes me thankful that he is toting my bags. Even though the bags roll, the extra weight and trying to keep them steady on the cobbled sidewalk would make me even hotter.

When I swipe my forearm across my wet forehead, I look at Jamie. She seems as cool as a cucumber. I wonder at her ability to handle the heat and humidity in this tropical locale. It doesn't help that I have worn a business suit to travel in. My mother always considered flying to be a special occasion. Her insistence that we dress up for plane rides sticks with me to this day, despite the fact that nearly everyone else dresses for comfort on flights.

We finally make it to a row of small apartments at the edge of the huge resort. Shay whips out a key and unlocks the door for one of them. "Voila!" He says as he uses his arm to usher us inside.

To call the makeshift room 'bare-bones' would be overly kind. The sparse space consists of a tiny twin bed with a paper-thin mattress, a rickety bedside table with a lamp, and a door that I hope leads to a private bathroom.

I try not to let the disappointment show on my face as I take it in, but it must be obvious because Shay says, "I know it's not much."

"No, it's great," I lie, forcing my face to form a smile.

Jamie gives me a questioning gaze, like she wonders if I can possibly be telling the truth.

"It's not great." Shay calls me out on the lie. "But it will give you a safe, dry place to sleep."

He flicks a switch and the ancient, wobbly ceiling fan groans to life. It is so decrepit looking, I wonder if it will stay attached to the ceiling or fall down onto the bed.

When it manages to stay up there, it dawns on me that this light stirring of the humid air is the only cooling mechanism for the room because there is no air conditioner. I will probably melt into a puddle of sweat.

Refusing to be ungrateful, I turn to Shay. "You have saved my day. Thank you."

"You're quite welcome." He gives me a flirtatious smile, but I refuse to be charmed. I'm here to help Ruthie, not to have a steamy fling with a hot islander.

Holding the door open and ushering them out with an unsubtle gesture of my hand, I say, "Good day."

If they are startled by my abruptness, neither shows it. They make a quick exit, and I shut the door behind them, glad to finally be alone.

I am pleased to see the room's interior door indeed leads to my own bathroom. After I make use of it, I catch a glimpse of my reflection in the tarnished mirror over the sink. I had forgotten what a swirling rat's nest my hair is from the cab ride.

No wonder Shay balked at the idea that he would have a fling with me. I look like a ridiculous hot mess.

Flopping down on the bed, I let the tears flow. It has been tough facing head-on Ruthie and Baggy's hatred of me, and this day has been less than stellar.

After my crying jag subsides, I swipe the sleeve of my business jacket across my cheeks. Telling myself to suck it up, I realize that this trip can only get better from now on... *Right?*

6

*T*he fact that the shower in the room Shay has loaned me only heats up to lukewarm is probably a blessing in disguise. I love to stand under a steamy, piping hot spray and let it relax my tense muscles, but that wouldn't be the brightest move on this tropical island. Even though the water is tepid at best, the humid air has me sweating again as soon as I emerge from the bathroom.

I wrap the room's only towel--which I'm hoping is clean--around me and vow to never take air conditioning for granted again.

Unable to stand the thought of my blow dryer, I decide to let the humidity take control of my unruly curly hair. I don't bother with makeup, other than sunscreen and mascara, because the heat would melt anything more off in a matter of minutes. It won't be the best look for my world-wide television show debut, but some things simply can't be helped. Besides, this isn't about me.

It's about Ruthie and Andrew. The only thing that matters to me is making sure that their big day goes perfectly.

When I venture out of the room in search of the others, I am pleased to find that the resort's pool and beach area is absolutely gorgeous. I was so focused on following behind Shay earlier that I didn't bother to stop and take note of the hotel's stunning beauty.

There are several interconnected pools with people of all ages and sizes whooping it up in the cool blue water. The infinity pool that overlooks the ocean, the waterslides that land in the deep pool, the swim-up bar, the kiddie pool, and the splash pad all work together to make this tropical paradise the perfect location for families to enjoy a relaxing, fun day.

I don't see anyone from the show, so I follow the call of the pristine beach. After removing my sandals, my tootsies are thrilled to find that the light-colored, fine-grained sand is cool to the touch. I am able to walk along the edge of the water barefooted with no troubles.

I still don't see anyone from the show, but I do find a familiar face. Walking over to the water-sports rental hut, I shield my face from the sun with one hand and smile at Shay. "Hi."

"Oh, hi!" He responds with a lot more enthusiasm than I showed.

"So, this is where you work?" It's a dumb question because it's obviously true, but I'm trying to hide my shock that a grown man actually does this for a living. I don't want to sound like a snob, but he can't possibly consider this to be a rewarding career. *Can he?*

Ignoring my admittedly bitchy tone, Shay beams at me and confirms. "This is my office. It's much better than a cubicle. Wouldn't you agree?"

Deciding it's really not my place to judge, I give him one brisk nod. Changing the subject, I ask him, "Have you seen anyone else from the show? I can't seem to find them."

He looks surprised by my question. "Oh, didn't anyone tell you? They are all at the welcome buffet in the main dining hall."

Feeling miffed, but trying not to let it show, I say, "No. I guess they forgot to mention it to me. Thanks for the tip."

"Anytime," he says to me, even though I have already started walking in the direction of the resort's main building. Now that he has mentioned food, my stomach is growling. I know that my body treads a very thin line between a little bit peckish and ravenously hangry. Shay shouldn't have to see my hulk-like transformation––no one should.

Calling after me, Shay says, "Hey, Lizzie?"

I don't want to linger out here when my tummy is demanding access to the hot buffet, but I stop and turn to see what he wants.

"You look so much better in that sundress than you did in that stuffy business suit."

I think he intends for his words to be a compliment, but it is at best a backhanded one. I scrunch up my face to let him know I'm unsure of his intent. "Umm... thank you?"

He has to have heard my questioning tone, but he still responds, "You're quite welcome."

Deciding that this professional beach bum's opinion is the last thing I need to be worried about, I saunter off without a second glance in his direction.

By the time I reach the restaurant, the hotel's staff is closing the buffet line. I scurry forward. "Wait, please wait." I beg them. "I haven't eaten yet."

"This is only for cast and crew members with the show," a grouchy looking woman in black pants and a starched white shirt informs me.

I feel like rolling my eyes. Am I going to face this same problem at every turn?

Jamie comes to my rescue by confirming to the grump, "She's with us."

The woman scowls and continues clearing away the metal food trays, despite the fact that she reluctantly tells me to "Have at it."

I fill my plate with what I can grab before she whisks it away. To say the food is picked over is the understatement of the year, but I take a seat in the near-empty restaurant and scarf it down like a starving woman.

"Sorry about that." Jamie apologizes as she slides into the seat beside me. "I thought you decided to sleep rather than eat."

"I did doze off for a few minutes," I admit before adding with a smile, "But food always takes priority in my life."

Jamie chuckles at my lame joke before adding, "Same."

The other members of the cast and crew have finished up and most have moved on. Jamie stays to keep me company as I eat, and soon we are the only ones left in the giant hall, other than the restaurant staff.

"Look, I really owe you one for earlier." Jamie sounds sincere. It makes me wonder what would have happened if I had pitched a fit about not having a room. Surely, T.J. wouldn't fire her over one tiny slip-up like that, would he?

She seems to be expecting a response, so I say around a bite of lukewarm fried shrimp, "You don't owe me anything."

"Well, you saved my butt, and now you're stuck in that horrible little room."

I am relieved to hear her say how awful the room is. I don't want to sound like a diva, but sparse is too generous of a description for my accommodations. "It's not that bad," I try, which makes us both burst into hysterics.

Once her laughter begins to subside, Jamie says, "Here's a free tip for you. Do not go into any of the resort's regular rooms. It will only make you see what you're missing."

"I'll keep that in mind." I smile at her, knowing the guest rooms are probably plush, boasting both air conditioning and hot water.

Jamie and I share a warm moment as we beam at each other, and I suddenly realize how much I have missed having the friendship of another woman. Roxy and Ruthie had always filled that vital role in my life. Now that they no longer wish to be that close to me, their absence creates an aching void in my chest.

Since Roxy and I have been friends since preschool, and Ruthie was a package deal with her sister, I have no idea how to go about the process of making a new friend. Many of the other employees at my office are bitter that I moved up the chain so quickly to work alongside the CEO. He treats me as a true peer, rather than a subordinate, and it ruffles a lot of feathers. Not knowing who is angry and whispering behind my back has made me rather aloof with my co-workers.

It feels like I am on the verge of forging a real friendship with Jamie, but we need some type of nudge to push us over the edge. Deciding to go the brutally honest route, I say, "Look, I don't have any friends here––or at home." I look down when I admit the last part. "I would love it if we can become friends."

Jamie looks stunned. I wonder if I have been too forward until she finally says, "Really? That would be great!"

With that, our friendship is sealed. Considering that the Rose family is still being overly cautious of me and that the producers of the show are bound to pull all kinds of stunts to try to ruin the wedding, it will sure be nice to have a friendly face in my corner of the ring.

7

*J*amie takes me to where the crew has set up and is filming for the day. One of the resort's pools has been cleared of any other guests, and blocked off for the production. Ruthie is wearing giant black sunglasses and a huge floppy hat as she basks in a lounge chair. She already looks like a pampered movie star.

Andrew and the rest of her family are scattered about in the shade, drinking frozen concoctions with cute colorful paper umbrellas hanging over the sides. It dawns on me then that we are missing some vital people for the wedding.

Turning to Jamie, I ask, "When are Roxy and Andrew's family arriving?"

"They'll get here the day right before the wedding. For the pre-shots, they wanted to just include the happy couple and the bride's parents. Baggy insisted on coming early, but her husband will have to come when Roxy and the others do because he has 'important spy business' to take care of before his arrival."

Jamie makes air quotes with her fingers and closely watches for my reaction to Baggy's outlandish belief that she and her husband are spies. I turn to smile at my new friend. "I love Baggy with all my heart." I preface my opinion because I don't want it to sound too judgmental or mean. "But it sounds to me like Baggy may have found someone to marry who is just as crazy as she is."

Jamie looks relieved that she isn't the only one who thinks Baggy's spy talk is a little over the top. "Match made in heaven," she agrees.

As if our talking about her has summoned her, Baggy clomps up to the edge of the pool. She is decked out from head to toe in Nike gear, including high top tennis shoes that are at least three sizes too big for her. She even has a Nike headband holding back her white curls. Between the high tops and the overly long, silky basketball shorts, an inch of bluish white skin is peeking out.

Ruthie glares up at the sleeveless team jersey Baggy is sporting. "What on earth are you wearing?"

"It's called product placement," Baggy stage-whispers her answer. "I'm going to have all kinds of sponsorship deals and commercial offers when this show ends."

Turning to face one of the cameramen, she tells him to zoom in for her close-up. She waits a moment for him to comply, before adjusting the volume of her voice to be loud enough to carry clear across the pool. "I only wear Nike clothes, shoes, and undergarments." She pauses after the last word to waggle her sparse gray eyebrows into the camera lens.

The entire group gapes at her as she continues. "If you want to be a sexy winner, like me, insist on only the Nike brand."

Once she finishes her spiel, she juts out one hip and preens for the camera. Ruthie is rubbing her temples as if she is getting a headache.

Caroline snaps at her mother, "That's quite enough of that."

Baggy turns stunned eyes on her daughter. "We'll see how you feel when my millions of dollars from endorsements start rolling in, and I don't share a penny of it with you."

Ruthie watches the entire exchange. Just when I think she is going to step in to smooth things over between her mother and grandmother, she shifts the attention back to her self by asking in a rather screechy tone, "Will someone please bring me two aspirin and a chilled bottle of sparkling water?"

Jamie hops into action to track down the requested items, and I stand there wondering if we are going to have a bridezilla on our hands.

Baggy calls after Jamie, "Make it Perrier, please." Turning to Ruthie, she stage whispers, "Maybe you can strike your own deal with them. We're going to be rolling in cash."

The old woman hoots with gleeful laughter over her silly plan. She cackles so hard that she doubles over to put her hands on her knees.

Everyone else goes back to what they were doing, but I keep my eyes on Baggy. Something seems off about her--more than her usual wackiness.

When she stands back up after her laughing fit, she wavers a little and places a hand over her chest. "Phew, I'm short of breath from cracking my bad self up."

I'm still staring at her, trying to assess if she's okay. The last thing I want to do is create a scene unnecessarily, but Baggy seems out of sorts.

When she begins to crumple to the ground, I am the first one to react. I lunge forward and reach her just in time to keep her head from hitting the concrete.

After gently lowering her the rest of the way to the ground, I make eye contact with a crew member that I haven't met before. Ordering him firmly, I say, "Call 9-1-1, or whatever the emergency service number is for this island. I think she's in cardiac arrest."

8

*A*s soon as I see the show's crew member digging in his pocket for his cell phone to call for emergency help, I spring into action. I'm so thankful for the CPR classes I took when my office offered them as an extra benefit. My reactions are automatic. I don't even have to think about them. My only goal is saving this wonderful woman, who has been my grandmother-by-choice for most of my life.

As I'm singing the classic Bee Gee's song "Stayin Alive" in my head to time the compressions and breaths, I'm vaguely aware of the others standing around and watching the horrific scene unfold. I hear Ruthie quietly sobbing in the background as Andrew attempts to comfort her.

I work tirelessly pumping the woman's tiny chest and forcing life-sustaining breaths into her lungs through her mouth. It seems like an eternity, but in actuality it probably isn't more than a few minutes.

During one of my compression cycles, I yell up towards the man who called for the ambulance. "Is help on the way?"

"Yes, they're coming," he promises me.

My arms are starting to get tired, but I will never stop. I can't risk losing Baggy.

Shay's calm voice is like a beacon in the night. "I know CPR. Would you like for me to take over?"

"No, I'm fine." I tell him––unwilling to hand Baggy's fate over to anyone, other than a medical professional.

Refusing to take no for an answer, Shay kneels down beside Baggy's tiny body. "You must be getting tired. At least let me do the compressions."

After nodding my head, I lean down to breathe into Baggy's mouth. As soon as I finish, Shay smoothly begins giving her perfectly-timed chest compressions. We work together like a well-oiled machine, completely in sync with each other's movements.

Eventually, we hear the siren in the distance. Once the cavalry arrives, the EMTs quickly and efficiently get Baggy onto a stretcher and into the ambulance. They have taken over our CPR ministrations.

The rest of the gang bolts into action as the ambulance takes off with its siren wailing. I sit back on my heels and finally let the panic and shock creep in. Putting a hand over my face, the frightened tears burst out.

Shay puts a comforting arm around my shoulders. I lean into his warmth. "She is going to be okay… Thanks to you." He soothes me.

I ache to believe his promise, even though I

know there is no way he can know it to be true. The mere idea of a world that doesn't include wild, wonderful, and wacky Baggy chills me to the core.

Evidently, I shiver at the thought because Shay puts his other arm around me, wrapping me into a comforting hug.

"Thank you so much for helping me." It dawns on me then that this man has assisted me with two challenging predicaments during my short time on this island.

"Of course," he brushes off my appreciation. "I'm happy to help you."

Since there is probably mascara running down my cheeks, I swipe my fingers under my eyes in an attempt to clean up my face a little. It dawns on me then that the others are probably waiting on me to get transportation to the hospital.

"I need to go check on Baggy." Rather than waiting for Shay's response, I stand up and bolt towards the lobby of the hotel.

Once there, I'm surprised to not see our group gathered there waiting for a ride. Spying the concierge, I ask him about securing a ride to the hospital for several people. As I'm trying to do a mental calculation of how many of us there are, he asks me, "A second one? Because we just had a big group leave in the shuttle van a couple of minutes ago."

Swallowing my hurt feelings that they hadn't waited on me, I reply, "Oh, then I guess I just need a ride for one."

"I can give you a ride in my Jeep," Shay offers

from behind me. I hadn't even realized he had followed me.

I'm touched that this man seems to always show up at the perfect time to help me out of a jam, so I try to insert appreciation into my smile when I turn to face him. "That isn't necessary. You've already done more than enough."

"I'm going there anyway." He insists as he puts an arm around me and steers me away from the concierge desk.

"You are?" I don't quite believe that he was intending to head out to the hospital, and I don't want to owe him any more than I already do.

"Of course," he furrows his brows together as if he is surprised I would ask such a thing. "I want to see how Baggy is doing."

Realizing that we are wasting precious time standing here arguing about it, I say, "Okay, I would love a ride."

It's not very far to the island hospital. Shay and I ride in silence. I am too anxious to make small talk, and he seems content with the quiet.

Once we get there, he lets me off at the door, and I bolt inside while he parks his Jeep. It doesn't take me long to find the large group of people in the waiting room.

As soon as I walk up to them, Ruthie engulfs me in a hug. "Your quick thinking and actions saved her. We will never be able to thank you enough."

I brush off her praise and ask how Baggy is doing.

It's Caroline that answers me. "We don't really

know. They won't let us see her, and they won't give us an update on her condition."

The volume of her voice rises in frustration at the end of her statement, and she is glaring at the gatekeeper behind the desk near the waiting room. I sense that these two have already had words.

Trying a different tactic, I walk up to the harried woman at the desk. Forcing a smile, I say, "Hi, If we can get an update on Baggy's condition, we would appreciate it. We are all so worried."

It feels weird to ask the woman about 'Baggy,' but despite how close I have been to her for most of my life, I don't know Baggy's given name. I'm sure that she has figured out who I am referring to by her previous interactions with our boisterous gang of family and television crew.

The woman's face softens slightly. "You will be updated as soon as possible. The doctors are still with her, but they will come out to talk to her family once she is stabilized."

I sag forward and let my shoulders slump upon hearing that Baggy still isn't stabilized.

Suddenly, Shay is behind me. I feel his warm, calming presence at my back. He puts an arm around me and guides me over to sit down with the others.

When we approach, Ruthie pats the seat beside her. "Lizzie, sit right here."

And just like that, I am accepted back into the family folds.

9

*I*t seems like an eternity as we wait for any news on Baggy's condition. I ask if the family has taken care of notifying Baggy's husband and Roxy. Caroline assures me they are both on their way. We spend the time in the waiting room regaling the show's crew members with crazy Baggy stories.

Ruthie gives us a watery smile, as she says, "It's a wonder she has lived this long with her horrible diet. She thinks Cheetos are cheese-adjacent enough to be a serving of dairy and that carrot cake counts as a vegetable."

"Don't forget how she thinks she gets plenty of vitamins from fruit-flavored Jell-O." I toss out.

"Remember that time Mother tried to secretly blend vegetables into her brownies? Baggy tried to spit a mouthful of them across the table when she found out, but her false teeth came out, too." Ruthie reminds me.

The gathered crowd, including some people

who are waiting on other patients, laugh at Baggy's nutty antics as we share them.

Ruthie's husband-to-be, Andrew, channels his nervous energy into perfecting a few magic card tricks, but most of us are too worried to appropriately react to them––even though they are quite good.

Shay waits patiently and quietly by my side. I discover that I am starting to like his calming presence, but I quickly remind myself not to get used to it. There is no room in my structured life for a man whose highest career aspirations involve basking on the beach and renting watersports gear out to tourists.

Finally, a doctor in puce green scrubs emerges from the double doors that separate us from the patients. "Margaret Elizabeth's family?" She asks.

I am stunned when Caroline stands. Baggy's real name is so fancy and formal. It doesn't suit Baggy at all. It's no wonder that no one uses her given name.

We all wait with bated breath for the verdict from the doctor. The woman trains her tired eyes mostly on Caroline, but still manages to seem like she is speaking to each of us individually.

"It was touch and go for a while. Margaret suffered cardiac arrest. It's a good thing someone started CPR so quickly. That person saved her life."

Ruthie grabs my hand within her own and squeezes it.

Evidently sensing how much she has lifted our hopes, the doctor's face turns grim. "She's not out of the woods yet, though. We'll need to closely monitor her for the next couple of days."

"Can we see her?" Ruthie asks with her eyes filled with hope.

"Just for a couple of minutes," the doctor responds. When the group collectively begins to perk up, she adds, "And only *immediate* family."

I'm devastated to hear this because I'm desperate to see Baggy, but I try not to let it show on my face. Ruthie's father stands to put an arm around Caroline. Ruthie turns first to Andrew, then to me and says, "Let's go." We both stand and follow her without question.

As we follow the doctor, my heart feels like it might swell right out of my chest at the realization that Ruthie once more considers me to be family. The constant ache that had been burning a hole into my heart for months begins to ease a little.

After we quietly enter Baggy's room, we circle around her bed. The diminutive woman seems so frail as she rests on her hospital bed attached to all kinds of beeping contraptions and IVs.

She peeks her eyes open to peer out at us. When her gaze lands on me, she asks, "What is *she* doing here?"

Her voice sounds feeble and croaky. Not wanting to upset her, I start to turn and quietly leave.

"Stay." Ruthie tells me before turning to Baggy. "She saved your life, Baggy. You went into cardiac arrest while we were filming by the pool. Lizzie took charge and performed CPR on you to keep your blood and air flowing."

"She did?" Baggy seems bewildered by Ruthie's

speech, and I wonder how much the doctor has shared with her about her emergency situation.

Ruthie nods and goes on. "Lizzie was a real hero."

I feel tears welling at Ruthie's high praise, but something compels me to brush it off as not being a big deal. "I just did what anyone else would do in the same situation."

Caroline reaches across Baggy's bed to take my hand within her larger one. It is an uncharacteristic affectionate gesture, and I gladly accept it. She reminds me kindly, "But you're the one who did it."

"Yep," Ruthie confirms, "Lizzie and that hottie watersports guy, Shay, saved the day."

"Hottie?" Andrew asks her, but he's smiling, obviously teasing.

"Not as hot as you," Ruthie assures him, leaning her head on his shoulder.

Baggy lifts one of her gnarled fingers in my direction, letting me know to come closer. When I do, she says sincerely, "Thank you, sweetheart."

It is an intense, emotional moment. I feel overwhelmed by the forgiveness I see in this family's eyes. For so long, I have been trying to figure out a way to make up with them for my momentary lapse in judgment. Now that it has happened, overjoyed doesn't begin to describe my level of happiness.

Proving that she can't be serious for too long, Baggy adds, "I hope that handsome fellow was the one who gave me mouth-to-mouth."

We all chuckle at her characteristic boldness.

Smiling down at her, I say, "Nope, sorry. That was all me."

"Well, dagnabbit." She responds.

Ruthie and I share a look over her odd word choice. Baggy isn't generally one to shy away from curse words.

Proving that she's as with-it as ever, Baggy sees our non-verbal exchange and explains. "I had one of those epiphadillies, while I was unconscious."

We all look at each other, trying to figure out what she means.

Andrew is the first to figure it out. "Do you mean an epiphany?"

"Whatever," she waves him off as if her first try made perfect sense. "I saw the big white light and it told me not to cuss any more. It's not ladylike. Besides, I don't want to be censored on the show. The world needs to hear my brilliance exactly as it is stated."

"I am in full agreement," I tell her sincerely. "The world needs more Baggy, live and uncensored."

Smiling, the older woman asks us, "Now, when can I get the fu-doodle out of here?"

I hear a shuffling noise behind us. When I turn, I realize for the first time that a cameraman and T.J. are in Baggy's hospital room with us. It is beyond me how they have managed to sneak back here, but it seems highly inappropriate for them to be taking advantage of Baggy's health crisis by filming in her hospital room.

T.J. turns to the cameraman and asks, "Did you get all of that? This will be ratings gold."

His brashness appalls me. I am just getting ready to give him a piece of my mind when Baggy fluffs her tight silver curls. "Do I look okay for my close-up?"

At our collective nods, she says to Ruthie, "Will you get my lipstick, dear? I don't want to look washed out on camera."

Ruthie complies. Once Baggy is satisfied with her looks, she stage-whispers, "Will someone please bring me a Diet, Caffeine-Free, Cherry Dr.

Pepper? It's the *only* beverage I drink." She winks directly at the camera.

Turning to us, she adds, "You need to be very specific in order to get a sponsorship deal. But don't be stealing my idea. You figure out something of your own to pimp out for money."

We smile amongst each other, realizing that the outspoken and outlandish Baggy we all know and love is still here with us.

Before long, a nurse comes in to shuffle us all out of the room, indicating that the patient needs to rest.

Baggy nods, before adding for the camera, "I need my beauty rest and some Olay Regenerist Eye Cream to look my very best. You can look this good, too, if you use it."

As the cameraman is backing out the door, she blows an over-exaggerated kiss at his lens. As we walk back to the waiting room as a group, it dawns on me how much I love that cuckoo woman. I don't want to imagine a world without her eccentric presence in it.

Caroline takes charge of making the announcement to the group we left in the waiting room. Clearing her voice to get their attention, she speaks in a loud, clear voice. "Baggy gave us all quite a scare, but she is already sharing off-color jokes and getting back to her unconventional version of normal. While the medical staff here is only cautiously optimistic, I have no doubts that Baggy will make a full recovery. The doctors here just don't know yet what a stubborn old broad she is."

"They'll find out soon enough," Ruthie's father quips, which makes us all chuckle.

Ignoring that, Caroline goes on. "Feel free to go back to the resort. There isn't any reason for all of us to be here. We will pass along any updates on Baggy's condition as we get them."

Even though she has effectively dismissed half the waiting room, nobody moves a muscle. Apparently, Baggy is so beloved by the entire group that we would all rather sit in an uncomfortable hospital waiting room in an attempt to show our support for her, rather than spending time at the luxurious tropical resort where we are staying.

Although no one explicitly states it, it is understood that we are all here for the long haul. We begin taking shifts where a portion of the group goes back to the hotel to shower and sleep, but everyone returns to keep vigil as close to Baggy as we can.

Only a couple of shifts have gone by when Baggy's frazzled husband, Howard, scurries in to join us. His thick gray hair is pointing out in every direction as if he has been repeatedly running his hands through it.

"Is she okay?" He asks as his eyes frantically search ours for answers.

"It looks like she's going to be," Caroline assures him before adding, "But she gave us quite a scare."

"I was on a top-secret mission someplace far from here, but I got here as fast as I could." He justifies his tardy arrival.

It dawns on me then that Baggy has found her perfect counterpart in Howie. I'm not sure if

59

either of them actually believes the wild spy stories they tell, but they both enjoy sharing the tall tales.

Suddenly turning serious and dropping the spy shtick, Howie's eyes water as he pleads with us, "Nothing can happen to her. I can't handle losing her. She's the best thing that ever happened to me."

I'm so happy that Baggy has found someone who loves her this much. It leaves hope for the rest of us that we might someday find that kind of happiness with someone. If crazy Baggy found her perfect mate, there must be someone out there for me. Right?

Not long after Howie's arrival, Roxy comes rushing in. She looks worried, but as beautiful as ever. Her skin is sun-kissed and glowing. Once we give her the rundown on Baggy's condition, we all comment on how the fragrant, tropical air in Hawaii must be good for her because she looks positively radiant.

It's the first time I have seen Roxy in person since before her ill-fated wedding day when I accidentally stole her groom. We have spoken on the phone and via email. She claims to have forgiven me, but I know today will be the true test of that.

After she has made the rounds of hugs and quick chats with her family, she ends with me. I'm surprised when she pulls me to her for a tight hug. When she whispers, "You saved her," near my ear, I know Ruthie has already shared that tidbit of news with her.

"She's like my grandma, too," I remind her.

She nods and sits down beside me. Ruthie joins us. Soon, the three of us are chatting and laughing, just like old times. It feels so good to be back inside the Rose sisters' circle.

"I missed you guys so much." I practically gush.

"We missed you, too." Roxy reaches out to hold my hand in hers.

Not wanting to get too mushy, I ask her, "So, when do I get to meet this handsome husband of yours?"

The smile that spreads across Roxy's face is filled with love as she thinks of Kai. "He's flying in right before the wedding. He runs a busy resort, so he feels like he isn't able to take too much time off work."

I nod, fully understanding the workaholic gene. Usually, I suffer from it, too, but I couldn't pass up this opportunity to make amends with Roxy and Ruthie.

Leaning in to whisper just loud enough for Ruthie and I to hear, Roxy asks, "What's up with you and the sexy surfer over there? He keeps giving you googly eyes."

"Oh, he does not." I try to brush off her observation, but Ruthie won't allow it.

"He's all about her." Ruthie inserts, nodding vigorously. "He's been panting around after her since we arrived. He even jumped in to help her with Baggy's CPR, and he's been keeping vigil by her side since Baggy was admitted to the hospital."

Roxy raises her eyebrows, obviously intrigued by these tidbits. "Really?" she asks, her tone dripping with interest.

"No," I shake my head. "He just let me stay in his room when I needed one. I think he's a genuinely nice guy, and he wants to make sure everything works out with Baggy's health."

Both women have their mouths open as they gape at me. It suddenly dawns on me what they must be thinking. "He's not in the room, you perverts. I barely know him."

"You know enough," Ruthie shrugs her shoulders.

"Yeah, it sounds like he's a pretty great guy," Roxy weighs in.

I look over at Shay. He is chatting with Andrew, since Ruthie and I are now busy with Roxy. Shay looks like a toned athlete. He is handsome, kind, sexy, and sweet, but he also has no ambition, and he lives way too far from me for us to make a relationship work.

"He's not the guy for me." I tell them with finality.

Ruthie narrows her gaze at me. "Nobody is saying you have to marry him, but I bet he'd make an unforgettable island fling."

I hadn't thought of that. Intrigued, I look at Shay again. Turning back to Ruthie, I surprise us all by saying, "You know, I think you might be right."

11

I spend a fitful night tossing and turning in Shay's bed, rather than sleeping. As much as I'd like to think I could have a meaningless island romance with him and leave it at that, I know I just don't have it in me. I'm more of a firm, long-term commitment kind of lady.

If I had my preference, I would spend the day at the hospital to be onsite for any news about Baggy, but Ruthie asks me to stay at the resort to represent her with wedding preparations. The cast and crew are back from their break in the hospital, and numerous details for the wedding, which will be streamed live, need to be dealt with. Apparently, the show must go on.

It is incredibly touching that Ruthie trusts me so implicitly with such a monumental event in her life. Plus, my job has trained me for this. I am the ultimate detail-oriented, multi-tasking, backup for my backup, prepare-for-the-unexpected queen, and I will not let her down.

Shay escorted me back to the resort last night and slept out on his boat. When I head down to take a walk on the beach before breakfast, I see him setting up the watersports hut, getting ready to open for business.

"Not heading back to the hospital today?" I ask him, silently wondering if he really was there just to keep me company, since this is the first day I'm not spending with my butt smashed in those hard plastic waiting room chairs.

"Nope, gotta get back to work." He flashes pearly white teeth in my direction.

Deciding to address it directly, I say, "I'm surprised you were able to take so much time off without any notice."

His ocean blue eyes search mine for a long moment before he says, "Some things are more important than work."

I nod, fully agreeing with that sentiment, but surprised that he feels so strongly for Baggy. She does tend to have that effect on people, but we really hadn't been here long when her emergency happened. I guess Baggy has so much charisma that it doesn't take any real length of time to grow to care deeply for her.

"I'm heading up to the restaurant to grab some breakfast. Would you like to join me?" It's a bold, uncomfortable question for me, but something about Shay makes me feel confident and carefree.

"I wish I could, but I need to get things going down here––especially since I haven't been around lately. Raincheck?" He sounds sincere.

Nodding and looking down at the light sand, I

try not to show my disappointment when I respond. "Sure. See you later."

"Bye, Lizzie." We spend a long beat beaming at each other as I realize that I love the way my name sounds rolling off his tongue.

Not wanting the moment to stretch into awkwardness, I finger wave at him and head towards the resort's main building.

As I'm filling a heaping plate at the impressive hot breakfast display, Jamie walks up behind me with a friendly greeting.

"Good morning." I smile back at her.

"I'm sitting over here," she points to a table with several other crew members, and just like that, it is understood that I am welcome to hang out with them today.

I bring my breakfast over to the boisterous table and slip into an available chair. It seems the discussion topic of the morning is T.J., since the man is nowhere to be found.

One of the cameramen says, "He wanted me to follow Andrew into the bathroom, but I drew the line at that."

This comment brings several chuckles from around the table because we all know how determined the producer is to get every usable shot.

A young lady who normally wears a headset jumps into the T.J. bashing. "You know he's probably going to try to get all of us to squeeze into Ruthie and Andrew's honeymoon suite after the wedding."

"Are we rolling? Don't miss this shot." One of the other cameramen mimics T.J.'s booming voice.

Jamie's quiet voice interrupts the revelry when she sticks up for T.J. "He's just trying to do his job and make sure we're all successful."

Her slight reprimand puts an end to the ridiculing of the producer. I study her face and am shocked to discover what I failed to notice before. She obviously has a major crush on T.J.

Now that the picking on T.J. has been effectively curbed, the group begins to disband. Soon, it is just Jamie and me left at the large table. She is done eating, but stays to keep me company while I finish.

I try to think how to bring it up without making her uncomfortable. Deciding that the direct approach is really the only way to go, I ask her, "What's up with you and T.J.?"

"What do you mean?" I don't fall for her innocent act because her eyes are gleaming with mischief.

Giving her a cut-the-crap stare, I say, "I have eyes."

"Okay," she chuckles, holding up her hands in mock surrender. "I might like him a little bit."

"A little bit?" I ask, fairly confident that she is significantly downplaying it.

She nods, but then admits, "Actually, I've been madly in love with him for years, but he doesn't know that I exist outside of work."

"How can that possibly be true? Is he blind?" I'm affronted that T.J. could shun my lovely and kindhearted new friend.

She smiles at me for immediately turning into a mama bear in her defense. "No, he just doesn't think of me in that way. It's not his fault."

With the beginning of an idea forming in my mind, I sit back and push my empty plate away. Grinning in Jamie's direction, I say, "Sometimes men need a little bit of a nudge."

12

*J*amie sounds alarmed as she chases after me, following me out of the restaurant. "What do you mean a nudge? You're not going to say anything to him, are you?!?"

Turning to face her, I realize that she is truly distraught. Softening my face, I say, "No, I would never do anything to embarrass you or risk your job. We're just going to make sure he sees what a desirable, fantastic woman you are."

Nodding her agreement that this might actually be a good idea, Jamie says, "Okay, but if you get to help me with T.J., I get to help you with Shay."

My first instinct is to deny any feelings for Shay, but she has just openly admitted her unrequited feelings to me. On a whim, I grin at her and say, "Deal."

With that our friendship is further sealed. Now that we have each other's backs, I decide to ask her if she knows what trials the producers have planned to add drama to Ruthie's wedding show.

Knowing I am putting her in a delicate position, I admit, "We are sort of at odds."

At her furrowed brow, I clarify. "You are trying to make a good television show, which means loads of mishaps and drama. I am trying to make sure Ruthie has a perfectly smooth, marvelous wedding."

"Oh, that." Jamie nods, confirming my suspicions that the show's bigwigs have some tricks up their sleeves to make sure the wedding isn't boring for viewers. "Actually, all of the drama so far hasn't been producer-created. Baggy's emergency will tug at viewers' heartstrings. That wild woman is beloved by all."

I nod, acknowledging that there is no way the producers could have planned Baggy's cardiac arrest. Scowling, I decide that they were probably secretly thrilled by the dramatic turn of events. Shaking my head to clear those anger-inducing thoughts, I refocus on Jamie.

"I know you can't risk your job, but if you could find a way to give me a head's up for anything that might ruin Ruthie's big day, I would so appreciate it."

Jamie nods, but remains quiet. I can tell the wheels are turning in her mind. Seeming to come to a decision, she whispers somberly, "Flowers, dress, and rings... And that's just what I've overheard."

"Oh my." I'm stunned they are planning to mess with so many elements of Ruthie's wedding. They evidently want her to have a total meltdown on screen. "Well, it sounds like I have my work cut out for me figuring out workarounds for any part of the wedding that might go wrong."

Jamie nods. Her face is drawn and somber as if she fears she might have just cost herself her job. Wanting to reassure her, I say, "I'll make sure no one finds out you gave me the tip."

The relief is immediate and obvious on her features. Wanting to make her feel even better, I add, "Now, what are we going to do to make T.J. notice you?"

My question has the opposite effect of what I was hoping for. Her expression falls and her brow furrows. "He'll never notice me. I've been quietly pining after him for years. He thinks of me as nothing more than a production assistant."

"Perhaps he's afraid of expressing an interest in you, since you work for him?" I try.

Slowly shaking her head, Jamie says, "He's not exactly known for being a rule follower." Her voice is filled with pride when she adds, "He's actually the mastermind behind all of the hijinks on the shows he hosts. He's so much more than just a producer or host. He's the brain behind the entire operation."

She's practically gushing about T.J. I don't particularly like the scheming, overly-slick man, but it's not my place to point out his flaws to her.

As if sensing where my thoughts have gone, Jamie rushes on. "He's not nearly as terrible as everyone thinks either. He actually cares very deeply for all of the cast members and crew. He just has a hard time showing it."

I nod, acknowledging that she believes him to

be a great guy––even if I don't yet see it myself. Sounding more confident than I feel, I tell her, "We'll figure out a way to get him to open his eyes to what a great catch you are."

There is no denying the hope overflowing from Jamie's gaze. "You think so?"

"I know so," I tell her, going all in with the calm, confident façade. I just hope I'm not setting us both up for disappointment.

13

*J*amie and I head our separate ways. She turns toward the large tent the crew has set up in the clearing near the beach, and I turn towards Shay's tiny room, so I can make a slew of online orders. Once I have backups on the way for everything I can think of, I finally begin to relax a little bit about the wedding. I'm confident that I can handle anything they decide to throw my way, and I won't let Ruthie's big day be ruined.

I feel at a loss over what to do until the staged wedding problems begin, so my feet somehow steer me towards the beach.

Shay is busy helping a tourist gear up with snorkeling equipment, so I walk along the water-side. Stopping to remove my sandals, I carry them and let the water splash up over my feet and ankles.

I'm not overly surprised, but am still very pleased, when Shay appears at my side. When he smoothly slides into my walking rhythm, I smile over at him. He is so easy to be with that things feel natural with him, almost like we have known each other for years, rather than mere days.

"Big plans for today?" He smiles down at me, and I suddenly realize the difference between him and most of the men I know. When Shay asks a question, he truly listens and seems to care about my answer, rather than it just being a perfunctory inquiry that is spoken only out of a misguided sense of politeness. Many times, I feel like men are waiting for me to be quiet so they can talk again. Shay doesn't in any way give me that impression.

"I'm sort of at a loss," I admit honestly. "I'm supposed to be running interference for Ruthie with the show's crew on wedding preparations, but they haven't started messing with her yet."

"Sort of the calm before the storm, huh?" He grins down at me, proving that he knows exactly the sort of tricks the producers will likely soon begin pulling.

"Exactly," I agree.

"Literally," he waves a hand out towards the flat, calm ocean.

I look out towards the sea. "What do you mean?"

He looks surprised by my question. "Oh, you haven't heard? There's a tropical storm tracking in our direction. If it stays on course, it will be here Saturday."

"The day of the wedding?" I screech.

At his confirming nod, the wheels in my mind start turning. "The producers might not have to create any drama for Ruthie's big day. Baggy's emergency and Mother Nature are taking care of it for them."

"It will be fine." Shay assures me, although I know there's no way he can know that. Proving that he's more intuitive than I would have thought, he goes on. "Ruthie and Andrew are obviously deeply in love. As long as the two of them are able to proclaim their love for each other in front of their family and friends, that is all that truly matters."

I nod, acknowledging that he is right about what is really important before adding, "I just want to make sure it's the perfect day for her."

"And that is what makes you such a lovely, wonderful person."

His high praise makes me uncomfortable. I know that my single-handedly––with some help from her groom––ruining of Roxy's wedding is sure to come out on the show. I don't want to see the look of disappointment in his eyes when he finds that out, but I decide it's better to fess up now than to have him find out when he watches the show.

"I'm not either of those things," I admit, shaking my head. "I've done some terrible things, and I owe Ruthie's family more than I can ever repay them."

"We've all done some terrible things." He tries to let me off the hook.

"You don't understand." I tell him sadly. My voice is so quiet when I continue, I'm not sure he'll hear me, but I can't stand to admit the biggest transgression of my life any louder. "I ruined Roxy's wedding day."

"I know." There isn't a trace of judgment in his tone.

I turn to look into his sea-blue eyes and find only true sincerity in his return gaze. The idea of this rugged, outdoorsy man watching reality television doesn't quite compute. I try to temper my tone when I ask, "You watched *Cruising for Love?*" The question still comes out more like an accusation than a sincere query.

"Of course." He chuckles when I'm unable to keep the shocked disdain off my face. "I'm kidding," he nudges my shoulder with his strong one. "Word spreads like wildfire among the employees at this resort. You and your friends were quite the hot topic when you arrived."

I hate the thought of him hearing gossip about my role in the demise of Roxy's wedding day. I would have much preferred to have the opportunity to tell him myself, so I could control the message a little bit. No matter what, it isn't a flattering story about me.

The concern over what he must be thinking about my character, or lack thereof, must be showing on my face because he puts an arm around me, effectively stopping our walk. He angles his body so he is able to look down into my face.

"There isn't a single person on earth who hasn't done something they regret, Lizzie." The way he is gazing at me like a surfer spying the perfect wave makes me uncomfortable. "You made a mistake, but you apologized for it, and you're doing everything in your power to make it up to

Roxy and her family. It's time for you to forgive yourself."

Shaking my head, I say, "I can't."

He leans down to press his lips against my forehead. His lips feel warm, soft, and comforting. It makes me wonder what they would feel like against my lips. When he pulls back, he tucks a stray strand of hair behind my ear. I have to force myself not to be completely enamored by the tender gestures, or the kind man administering them.

It would be too easy to fall for kindhearted Shay. I know myself too well to risk my heart on a man who lives the island lifestyle. There is no possible future where things could work out for us on a long-term basis.

"I'll help you see how worthy you are of mercy, forgiveness, and love."

His glorious words fill me with warmth. The high-pitched squeal of a drill securing a hurricane shutter pulls me out of my daze. I turn in the direction of the intrusive sound.

"Storm prep." Shay confirms for me.

The potential of a major storm invading our little island paradise the day of Ruthie's wedding creates another layer of potential issues that need to be anticipated and averted. Already making a mental checklist in my mind, I turn to Shay. "I need to go order more supplies."

He nods as if he already knew I wouldn't stay out on the beach for long. "Promise me one thing?"

Slightly irritated that he is keeping me from

my planning, now that it is taking over my racing mind, I nod to encourage him to spit it out.

"Take a lunch break and eat with me?"

"Okay," I nod and turn to head back to his room to get my laptop.

"You probably would have agreed to just about anything to get back to your planning. I should have asked for a kiss." He teases me.

I feel my cheeks burning hot at that thought, so I refuse to turn back to let him see how embarrassed I am by the delightful idea of him kissing me. Instead, I raise a hand behind me to wave goodbye to him as I scurry up the path away from the beach.

The wonderful sound of his deep laughter carries on the ocean breeze to follow along behind me.

14

*T*he knock at the door to my room startles me out of deep thought. I have lists, reminders, and purchase receipts on my computer. There are so many tabs open on my internet browser, the hotel's WiFi seems taxed to keep up with me. Each time I click on something it takes longer than the last time for the page to fully paint.

I fling the door open wide and am pleasantly surprised to see Shay on the other side. He is holding a picnic basket and a folded blanket.

"When you didn't show up at the restaurant for lunch, I decided to bring a meal to you."

I am incredibly touched by his sweet gesture, but it doesn't seem like it can possibly be lunchtime already. Glancing at the clock, I am stunned to see that it is already 1:45 p.m. As soon as I see the time, my stomach growls loudly. I put a hand over it to try to curb the sound and turn wide eyes in Shay's direction, hoping he didn't hear it.

He saves me from being too embarrassed by giving me a warm smile and saying, "Sounds like I'm just in time. Want to head down to the beach to eat?"

I nod, but sit back down on the bed and grab my computer. Justifying the maneuver, I say, "I just need to take care of a few things first. I'll meet you down there in a couple of minutes?"

Shay isn't willing to be brushed off so easily. "I'll stay while you save anything you need, but it's time for you to take a break and eat. You are on one of the most beautiful islands in the world, and you are spending your time inside a modest room staring at an electronic screen."

Somehow, his words don't sound as judgmental as they likely would if they had come from anyone else, but they still make me feel like a total loser. "I just want to make sure everything is perfect for Ruthie." I try to justify my hermit-like behavior.

"And it will be," he promises, even though there is no way he can possibly know that.

Walking over to stand in front of me, Shay sets the items he has been holding down on the foot of the bed and grins at me with kind eyes. "Have everything saved that you need?"

At my confirming nod, he gently takes the computer from my lap and closes it. I open my mouth over his brash move. He rationalizes his action by saying, "It will still be here when you get back."

Deciding that he is right, I stand up, plug the

computer in to charge, and pick up our picnic blanket. Shay grabs the heavy-looking wicker basket and we set off on our way.

Once we are settled on the blanket on the sand, Shay begins pulling all kinds of delicious-looking food out of the basket. My eyes widen as I watch the seemingly never-ending spread emerge.

Just as I'm thinking that my stomach is going to growl and embarrass me again, Shay grabs a plump strawberry, dips it in a tub of smooth chocolate and pops it into my mouth.

I practically groan at the delicious flavor. When the fruit juice drips down my chin, Shay uses the back of his finger to swipe it away. I feel uncomfortably warm deep in my belly, but in a good way, when he licks the juice off his finger. It's an oddly intimate move.

Shaking my head and searching for something to say, I finally land on, "No one has ever made a picnic for me like this before."

Shay shrugs his shoulders as if it isn't a big deal. "Stick with me, and I'll treat you like a queen."

I have no doubt that is the case, but I don't want to get too used to having him spoil me in this manner.

As he pours us each a glass of blush-colored, chilled wine, he adds, "Besides, I had a lot of help." Smiling sheepishly, he admits, "The kitchen staff loves me."

I don't want to acknowledge the flash of jealousy that spears through me as I wonder why the kitchen workers love him so much. My guess is that most of them are women. *Does he have a special relationship with one or more of them?*

Even though I know it's none of my business, the idea irks me. Unable to keep my hurt feelings completely under wraps, I say, "You don't have to babysit me, you know."

"Babysit you?" Shay's head has whipped back as if I have slapped him.

Nodding, I clarify. "It's probably part of your job to make sure the guests are happy and have a good time during their stay. You probably feel responsible for me, since I'm staying in your room."

Shay has the audacity to chuckle at my assumption. "I don't know what you think my job description includes, but I'm not a gigolo."

"I know that." I snap. I hadn't intended to imply that he was trying to sleep with me. When we first met, he clearly stated the fact that he wasn't willing to do that. I'm trying to convince myself that I'm not interested in a sexual relationship with him either, but there is no denying that I find it irritating that he is so opposed to the idea of it. *Aren't heterosexual men in the prime of their lives supposed to try to bed any remotely attractive, available females? Does he not even find me to be a little bit attractive?*

Almost as if he can read my thoughts, Shay reaches over and trails a finger between my eyebrows. "Why is this worry line making an appearance right now? You look so much lovelier when you allow yourself to relax for a moment."

I light up at his word choice. His implication that I am lovely, even with a frown line etched on my face, makes me beam as I stare out towards the rolling waves.

"It's gone." He confirms for me before adding, "I was right… You are positively gorgeous when you give yourself a second to breathe."

Uncomfortable with his praise, I look down and begin fiddling with making myself a ham and provolone sandwich on a baguette. Thrilled that his seemingly bottomless basket has everything I need, I swirl mayo and mustard together on the bread, just the way I like it.

I feel Shay looking at me, but I feel too awkward to acknowledge his gaze. When he says, "I bet that wild, curly hair drives you crazy," I try not to feel offended.

Smoothing my hands self-consciously over my unruly mane, I make a vain attempt to tame it. Knowing it's a lost cause, I admit, "I always wished for smooth, sleek, and sophisticated hair, like Roxy and Ruthie have, but it simply isn't meant to be for me. Even a flat iron doesn't quite hold up to my curls––especially not in this kind of humidity."

"I love your big, wavy hair. It's almost like you're wearing a sign right on top of your head that reminds you that you can't possibly control everything."

Chuckling, I decide he is right. I am a bit of a control freak, so having a giant mop of misbehaving curls drives me nuts. I prefer things orderly and in their place, but my hair refuses to comply. "I gave up trying to tell it what to do a long time ago." I admit to him.

"So, you are able to relax about certain things?"

His question sounds somewhat rhetorical but I

respond anyway. "Only after a long and hard battle of the wills."

Shay reaches out to wind a long tendril around his tan finger. "Maybe there's hope for me yet."

His words are so quiet as they are carried off on the sea breeze, I wonder if he actually uttered them or if it was simply wishful thinking on my part.

15

*S*hay and I eat in silence for a long while, savoring the beauty of the pristine beach, the sound of the waves rolling into the shore, and the sizzle of attraction that simmers just beneath the surface between us. The food is magnificent, and I eat way more than is probably socially acceptable for a first date--if that's even what this is.

Shay picks up a strawberry that is easily three times the size of an average one. I had been eyeing it, but try not to let the disappointment show on my face. After he dunks it in the milk chocolate fondue dip, I am thrilled when he holds it up to my lips. It's way too big to eat in one bite, so I take a nibble from the side. After that, he eats the remainder. It's a sensual move that makes me feel so squirmy that I shift on the beach blanket we are sharing. This man exudes sexuality without even seeming to realize it.

As we relax together after filling our bellies, I

ruminate over how different Shay is from anyone else I know. He never seems to have an agenda or want anything from me. It seems like he just genuinely enjoys spending time with me. If we don't happen to talk during that time, he's fine with that. It's so refreshing to spend time with someone who doesn't have any expectations of me.

"Want to go for a walk along the beach before we get back to work?"

I smile at him because that is exactly what I was just thinking. "Sounds marvelous."

He takes my hand to help me stand up from the sand, and I feel a surprising jolt from his touch. The best way I can think to describe it is a tingling extra-aliveness that I miss as soon as he lets my hand go. It dawns on me that I wish he had kept ahold of it for our walk, and that scares the hell out of me. The last thing I need is to fall for an island slacker who basks in a hammock all day and calls it work.

Wanting to be delicate, but feeling the need to bring it up, I turn to Shay and ask, "Is this where you see yourself five years from now––renting beach toys to tourists?" I know I have failed to keep the harsh judgment out of my tone.

He turns to tuck the lock of hair behind my ear that has blown into my face with the sea breeze. "Why do I feel like I've suddenly stepped into a job interview?"

His easy, wide smile lets me know that he doesn't have any hard feelings about my border-line rude question, but I can tell I have over-stepped.

Rather than holding a grudge about me sounding judgmental, Shay stops to pick up a bisque seashell before saying, "I'm happy. Are you?"

His direct question makes me uncomfortable. Happiness is something I don't really think about. I set goals for myself, and I achieve them. I try to live a good life, with the exception of my lapse of solid judgment right before Roxy's wedding. Other than lacking someone special to share the big triumphs and everyday moments with, my life is pretty great. I'm safe and financially secure. I'm close to my Mom, and I have now reconnected with Roxy and her family.

Slowly nodding, I decide to tell Shay that I am indeed happy, but he makes an obnoxious, nasally buzzer-type of sound. "Too late! If you have to think about it that long, you aren't truly happy."

"Yes, I am." I pout. "It just took me a while to process all of the reasons my life is so great."

Shay nods, quietly accepting my response, without further argument. After a long moment of us splashing through the shallow water, he says, "I'm glad. You deserve to be happy, Lizzie."

He is one of the most sincere, kind men I have ever met. It doesn't quite fit with the stereotype of the typical surfer dude that my mind continues to stubbornly cling to. Realizing that I haven't been fair to him, despite his consistent generosity and thoughtfulness towards me, I say, "You surprise me."

He raises sun-kissed eyebrows, making me realize that my statement is one that can easily be misinterpreted, so I clarify, "In a good way. You're amazing."

Now that I have flipped too far in the other direction and practically gushed over him, I feel my cheeks burning hot. Shay quickly lets me off the hook by responding, "You're the amazing one."

Looking down at the clear water ebbing and flowing over the light-colored sand, I shake my head, knowing that I am completely average in every way, with the exception of my almost obsessive-compulsive organizational skills.

Shay stops walking and turns to face me. Knowing it would be rude to continue on, I don't see another option except to stop and look up at him. His sapphire blue eyes match the ocean's hue as they sparkle down in my direction.

Once he has my full attention, he wows me with some of the most marvelous words that have ever been said to me. Taking both of my hands within his own, he says, "You are so naturally beautiful, and you don't seem to even have any idea. You are loyal to the point that you would do anything for your friends and family-by-choice–– even if it's not in your best interest. You are hard-working, almost to a fault."

He pauses to smile down at me, and I find that I can't hold his sincere gaze. Using a finger to lightly lift my chin, so that I am forced to look at him again, he continues, "You are incomparably generous and kindhearted."

At this, I can't let him go on without saying something. "You are the generous and kindhearted one. You gave me your room when I needed one, even though I was a complete stranger. At every turn, you are there to help me when I need it, even though I'm not your problem."

"You aren't a problem, but I wish you were mine."

I know it's probably a slick line that he uses to get gullible tourists into his bed, but my mouth falls open at his seductive words. My eyelids feel heavy as he gazes down at me, and I wonder if he is going to kiss me.

It's the perfect moment for a kiss. I find myself aching for the feeling of the brush of his lips against mine. His smooth words might be a practiced trick, but I can't resist the pull of him. I don't *want* to resist his magnetism.

We hover there together for a long moment. My face is tipped up in an open invitation for a kiss. He seems to be pondering the idea, trying to decide if it would be a mistake.

I wonder if I should rise up on my tippy-toes to close the tiny gap between us. Just as I am getting ready to do just that, Shay looks away and says, "I suppose it's time for us to head back. You probably have a to-do list a mile long for today, and I'm keeping you from it."

It's tempting to tell him that I would much rather stay out here with him, but I refrain. There must be some reason why he didn't take advantage of the ideal moment to kiss me. I don't want to seem desperate or clingy, so I smile and say, "Yep, I have lists of lists to accomplish."

With that, we turn and head back towards the resort. Our walk is silent, except for the sigh of disappointment that escapes my lips and is carried away by the crashing waves.

*J*amie and I are eating thick, juicy cheeseburgers and fresh-cut fries from the poolside shake shack. I'm still feeling a little bit down over Shay's decision not to kiss me, so I'm indulging in a cool and delicious chocolate milkshake, too.

"Maybe he was waiting for you to make the first move," Jamie suggests, obviously trying to cheer me up.

I give her a classic 'get real' look. "Does he look like the kind of guy who would be scared to kiss a woman that he finds attractive?"

"No," Jamie admits, before adding, "But maybe he respects you enough to not take advantage, since you'll be leaving in a few days."

I nod, silently admitting that she's right. "Normally, I would appreciate that because my logical mind can't compute how a relationship with Shay could possibly work out in the long-run, but something about him is so attractive."

Leaning in to share my secret with her, I whisper, "I think I might want to have an island romance with him."

The surprised look on Jamie's face is undeniable. Despite the short time we've been friends, she evidently knows a fling is out of character for me. Proving that she already knows me quite well, she asks, "Do you think you can handle that? Or will you beat yourself up about it when you get home?"

Nodding, I accept that she's probably right. "Yeah, I suppose I would. But it sure is fun to think about."

We grin at each other before Jamie adds, "He is a total babe."

I smack playfully at her arm before teasing, "Back off––he's mine! You have your own crush. How are things with T.J., anyway?"

Jamie's face falls. "The same. It's always the same. I secretly pine away for him from a distance, and he doesn't know I exist."

"We're going to change that." I vow, silently adding matchmaking to my mental checklist.

Our chat is interrupted when Ruthie comes running up to our table. Her eyes look heavy, like she hasn't been sleeping well, and her hair is uncharacteristically rumpled. "They are wanting me to move the ceremony inside because of the incoming storm."

Her beautiful gaze is practically frantic as she looks to me for help. I decide to test the waters by suggesting, "It might keep us all from blowing away."

"I've always dreamed of a picturesque beach

wedding, though. If we get married inside the hotel, we might as well have stayed home."

I nod to acknowledge that Ruthie has a point. "I'll take care of it." I promise her, even though I have no idea how I will be able to do that.

I savor the look of pure gratitude Ruthie gives me just before pulling me in for a heart-warming hug. In that moment, I decide I will stay up day and night until the wedding, if I need to, in order to figure out how to make Ruthie's dream wedding a reality.

As soon as I hear the prim, judgmental voice, I feel Ruthie's entire body stiffen in my arms. We pull away from each other and share a wide-eyed look. Ruthie's complexion is white as a sheet.

"Who invited her?" Her voice is barely above a whisper.

I don't have to turn and look to see who it is. I would know Roxy and Ruthie's paternal grand-mother's condescending voice anywhere. She's speaking to a limousine driver. "Take my bags up to my room."

This order is not accompanied by a please, thank you, or tip. Grandmother Rose just expects people to bend over backwards to do what she says, even if it's beyond their job descriptions.

Although the chauffeur appears to be a bit miffed, he complies with her request. When he's walking by, I hear him say to the concierge, "She's all yours. Have fun." His laugh carries down the hallway as he rolls the cart piled high with Louis Vuitton luggage.

Ruthie is frozen in place as if she can't quite believe this misfortune. Jamie is bugging her eyes out at us. I can tell that she was in on the decision to bring Ruthie's snooty grandmother here. "I'm sorry," Jamie hisses out the side of her mouth. "We thought it would be a good surprise to bring Ruthie's other grandma in for the wedding."

My guess is that Jamie truly thought it would be a pleasant surprise, but that T.J. knew exactly what kind of havoc her presence would wreak. Sensing that Jamie feels bad about her part in the unpleasant intrusion, I manage to quietly say, "Her arrival is rarely a good thing," before Grandmother Rose narrows her gaze and saunters over to us.

"Ruthie, darling," the woman air kisses the bride-to-be. "You look pale and tired. You need to get some rest, dear." Somehow, under the guise of being concerned, this woman has managed to insult Ruthie's appearance just before her wedding day.

My teeth clench together as I look at this hateful, prissy woman, who is so different from Ruthie's loving––if somewhat crazy––other grandma, Baggy.

When the icy blue eyes fall on me, it is all I can do not to fall back into my old habit of allowing my shoulders to slump forward under her harsh scrutiny. Instead, I force myself to stand tall and return her direct gaze.

"Lizzie." She finally greets me, but she spits my name out like I am a bug doing the backstroke in her water glass.

"Grandmother Rose," I say, feeling like an awkward teen again.

"I'm not your grandmother," she reminds me with a cool tone.

Ruthie attempts to cover for the woman's rudeness. "Lizzie has apologized for what happened at Roxy's wedding, and we have forgiven her, Grandmother."

"What happened at Roxy's wedding?" The woman asks, proving how clueless she is about her own family.

"Nothing," Ruthie immediately realizes her mistake and tries to quickly brush it aside.

I remember how relieved Roxy had been when Grandmother Rose had announced she wouldn't be able to make the trip up for Roxy's planned wedding to Gary because of the woman's annual country club fundraising ball, which she takes great pride in planning. I am surprised to hear that no one has mentioned to the older woman why the nuptials fell through, though.

Deciding to be thankful for small favors, I say, "Everyone will be so glad you are here." It's a lie, but I can't let the awkward silence drag on forever.

Proving that she knows exactly how disliked she is, but is unconcerned about it, the woman says sarcastically, "Right." Turning her perfectly made-up face towards Ruthie, she says, "It's a good thing I'm here, though. Someone has to make sure this wedding doesn't make us a laughing-stock, unlike that ridiculous show did last time."

The woman's unwavering gaze is trained on Ruthie. I would squirm under the pressure of it, but Ruthie manages to hold her own. She lifts her chin and says, "I got a second chance with the love of my life on that show, so I think that's worth having our family suffer a tiny bit of embarrassment."

"Tiny?" The woman's sparse gray eyebrows shoot up almost into her snow-white hairline. "I wasn't able to show my face in the club for weeks."

Needing to change the subject, I ask her, "Did you have a nice flight?"

She looks at me like I need a brain transplant. "No, dear. Are flights ever nice? This one was worse than normal, though. It was bumpy... even in first class."

I force myself not to scoff at her ridiculous cluelessness. *Does she really think first class on a plane can possibly be a smoother ride than coach?*

Jumping onto that excuse, Ruthie gives her a sympathetic expression that I can tell is fake. "That sounds dreadful." At the woman's nod, she adds, "Perhaps you should go lie down for a bit."

"I think I will." The woman easily slides into her comfortable role of pampered princess. "Will you have some Dom sent up to my room?"

"Of course," Ruthie nods as the woman finger waves at us and finally turns to leave.

As soon as she's out of earshot, Jamie asks incredulously, "She drinks Dom Pérignon in the middle of the afternoon on a random weekday?

"That's Grandmother Rose." Ruthie confirms as we all shake our heads and watch the spoiled woman walk away.

Jamie says, "I guess things just got a whole bunch more interesting."

"You have no idea." Ruthie and I say at the same time, which makes us all burst into hysterics.

know that Baggy and Grandmother Rose hate each other, but I had managed to forget how much venom there is between the two polar opposites.

"Oh, that ridiculous woman is here?" Grandmother Rose's face is pinched as if she has just tasted a particularly sour lemon.

"Of course," I smile, trying to smooth things over, even as I'm regretting my decision to join Grandmother Rose for dinner. The rest of her family is at the hospital, awaiting further news on Baggy, so I am trying to be kind and keep her from having to dine alone. Apparently, the old adage is true and listening to the bitter woman gripe about Baggy is my punishment for that good deed.

When Shay walks up to our table with his wide, friendly smile, I breathe an audible sigh of relief. As much as I don't want him to have to face her scrutiny, I need a break. "Mind if I join you?"

Grandmother Rose's thin brows snap together

as Shay goes ahead and takes an empty seat at our four-top table. Her lips are pursed when she asks, "Do I know you?"

It's a rhetorical question, meant to make him slunk away, but I step in and make the appropriate introductions before giving Shay an apologetic smile. He beams back to let me know he doesn't blame me for the other woman's rude behavior.

Seeming to accept that Shay is joining us, the woman turns her steel blue gaze in his direction. She eyes him from head to toe and quickly zeroes in on the one thing that bothers me about him. "What is it that you do for a living, young man?"

Shay remains unruffled by her scrutiny. "I help people enjoy their vacations," he responds as if he has the greatest job in the world.

"Sounds to me like you're a beach bum." I squirm in my seat as I realize that I am just as judgmental about Shay's vocation as this hateful woman is.

"I guess you could say that." Shay shrugs his shoulders, not caring a bit about her obvious disdain.

Unwilling to let it go at that, the older woman pushes on. "And you're satisfied with that? You don't have any higher aspirations?"

I lean forward, anxious to hear his answer to her questions. He avoided directly answering when I asked, but she won't likely let him off the hook so easily.

When Shay says vaguely, "I do okay," I feel disappointed. I had secretly been hoping he had some grand plan that he could whip out to dazzle us. It dawns on me then that this might truly be it for him. Now, I have to decide if that's enough for me.

Although I am critical of Shay's profession, I hate the sneer Grandmother Rose is giving him. She's looking at him as if he is beneath her and no longer worth any of her time. I feel an over-whelming urge to defend him. "Shay might not have high career aspirations." I cringe as I hear how harsh my own word choice sounds. All eyes are on me, so I feel in too deep to stop now. "But he is a smart, kind, and gentle soul."

Grandmother Rose scoffs as if my defense of him has made him seem even weaker in her eyes. "Don't tell me you're romantically interested in this slacker, Lizzie. I thought even you would have higher standards than this."

I can't believe this woman is saying such insulting things right in front of Shay. He looks completely unperturbed by the entire exchange, but I am fuming.

I can feel my eyes firing imaginary darts in the other woman's direction. "Shay is an amazing man, and any woman would be lucky to have him."

Shay's sparkling blue eyes are glued to mine when he asks, "Do you really think that?"

"Yes." I force my voice to remain clear, even though my heart has suddenly jumped into my throat.

Shay doesn't hesitate. He leans over and brushes his lips lightly across mine, right in the middle of the crowded restaurant.

I register Grandmother Rose's sharp intake of breath, but I don't care that we are shocking and offending her with our scandalous public display of affection. The only thing I can focus on is the delightful shiver emanating throughout my body from Shay's sweet kiss.

Too soon, he pulls back. I immediately miss the warm pressure of his lips against mine, and I can't keep the dreamy expression out of my eyes when they flutter open. We gaze at each other as if we are the only two people in the room, despite the bustling activity around us, and the judgmental huffs of disapproval from our tablemate.

Just as I'm thinking that I don't care if Shay builds sandcastles for a living, as long as he agrees to kiss my like that every day, Jamie rushes up to our table. Her distraught expression is one of the only things––short of an emergency––that could have pulled me out of my awestruck daze.

"They're putting together a pre-wedding show to air tomorrow night," she announces without preamble.

"Really? I'm surprised they have enough footage to cobble together a show." I feel my brows tug together. "They aren't going to exploit Baggy's medical emergency, are they?" Even though I know the show's producers tend to put an unflattering spin on everything, using Baggy's cardiac arrest to gain ratings would be overstepping the rules of common decency.

"That's the problem... I don't know." Jamie practically wails.

"You don't know?" Her announcement surprises me. "But I thought you were normally involved in every detail of the production."

"I usually am," she confirms before adding, "But they've completely taken me out of the loop."

Sitting down at the vacant fourth chair at our table, Jamie shakes her head and says, "This can't be good."

Patting her hand, I try to reassure her. "I'm sure it will all be fine." Even as I'm saying the words to her, the adage 'Famous last words' is echoing through my mind.

amie wrings her hands, obviously distraught that she isn't being included in the show planning. "Do you think I'm in trouble for sharing too much with you?"

"No," I assure my friend––even though we're both aware that there isn't any way I can possibly know that for sure. Trying to cheer her up, I suggest the best scenario I can think of. "Maybe they are working on a big surprise for you."

"Yes," Grandmother Rose scoffs before adding in a trilling voice, "Surprise! You're fired."

I glare at the hateful woman's obvious sarcasm, uncertain why she feels the need to be so mean all the time. One glance at Jamie's crestfallen face tells me that the older woman's sharp talons have hit their mark.

Shay jumps in to make Jamie feel better. "Why would they fire Jamie? By all accounts, she is the one who takes care of all of the details and keeps the production running smoothly."

It's my sentiments exactly, but it uplifts Jamie's spirits more coming from Shay, since he is more of an unbiased outside observer.

Deciding that the last thing we need is to sit around and let Jamie worry about what is coming, I suggest, "We should go to the poolside bar and have a celebratory drink."

"What are you celebrating––Jamie's last day of gainful employment?"

I feel like kicking the hateful old woman under the table, but somehow I manage to refrain. Instead, I smile and effectively dismiss the old bat by saying, "Have a nice evening."

When I rise to leave, Shay and Jamie both follow suit. Once we are out of earshot, Shay quips, "She's a bit of a mean old hag, isn't she?"

I'm not sure why it strikes me as being so funny to hear him state the obvious. Maybe it's because he normally gives everyone the benefit of the doubt. Hearing him speak so unkindly about her confirms my belief that the woman is truly despicable.

We grab a tall table near the bar and order frozen, fruity rum-based drinks that are adorned with little brightly-colored paper umbrellas. As soon as we empty our glasses, Shay bellies up to the bar for fresh ones. I've lost count of how many we've had when Jamie hisses a little too loudly, "T.J. is here."

The producer spies us just as I look over. I can tell the alcohol flowing through my veins is making me bolder than normal, but I seem unable to stop myself from bending my pointer finger to summon him in our direction.

Jamie bugs her eyes out at me when she realizes what I've done.

"Don't worry," I tell her, patting her hand awkwardly. "We're going to make him jealou-sh." My head tips to the side when I realize that my words aren't coming out quite right. "I mean jealou-sh." My repeat of the mispronunciation strikes me as incredibly funny, and I'm cackling with laughter when T.J. slides into the vacant chair at our table.

"Sounds like you are having a fun evening," he doesn't even attempt to keep the judgment out of his tone, but I am far too happy to worry about it.

"Oh, yeah," I confirm leaning over to beam a wide grin in Shay's direction. I wonder why he doesn't seem to be affected by the alcohol at all, but decide I must just be a lightweight because I so rarely drink. "We're having a blast, aren't we?"

Shay answers my question. "We sure are."

"Do you think you might kiss me again later?" Some part of my brain registers that I shouldn't be asking Shay such a bold question, but my mouth won't cooperate.

Shay is giving me an utterly amused smile. "I might," he confirms.

"You might?!?" My tone is filled with outrage. "I think you mean you *will*." I lean in with my lips puckered, thinking that he might fulfill my wish right now, but T.J. clears his throat.

Turning to look at him, I say, "Oh, right. You're still here."

When the idea pops into my mind, I know that

it is utterly brilliant. Turning to Jamie and waving my hand in the direction of the bar, I ask her, "Do you think that guy over there will send any more flirtinis over to you?"

"Umm, I'm not sure." Jamie seems uncertain what to do with my setup, so I go in for the spike.

Waggling a finger in T.J.'s direction, I say to him, "You better grab this gorgeous, brilliant young woman while you still can because men are lining up all over for a chance with her."

The swift kick under the table startles me. "Ow! What was that for?" I ask Jamie as I reach down to rub my shin.

Shay jumps in to stop things before they escalate. "Let's get you home," he suggests, standing and taking my arm.

"Ohhh, you want to do more kissing, eh?" I raise my eyebrows at him in what I hope is a suggestive maneuver, although it merely feels awkward.

"Something like that," he promises before telling the other two we will see them tomorrow.

Turning back, I yell over my shoulder at Jamie, "Go get him, tiger!" I try to give her a thumbs-up sign, but Shay is already shuffling me away.

Confused, I look up at him. "She gave me a dirty look. Did I do something wrong?"

"Nah," he tells me before adding, "I think maybe you just gave her more of a nudge than she was ready for."

"Hmph. Well, she needed it." I decide, thinking to myself what a great friend I am as Shay steadily guides me to his room that I have taken over since my arrival.

When we reach the door, I fumble with the key. He smoothly takes it and opens the door for me. I take his hand and try to pull him inside.

Shay stands his ground, refusing to step over the threshold into his room. "I think you need some sleep," he suggests.

"First, I need some kissing," I grin up at him before resting my head on his broad shoulder. Wrapping my arms around him, I murmur, "You're so warm."

"And you're so drunk." His tone doesn't sound in the slightest bit accusatory. He is simply stating a fact.

"Just a little tipsy," I admit, holding up my finger and thumb a fraction of an inch apart.

Shay returns my embrace with his strong arms. "I won't take advantage of you when you're a little tipsy." He uses my own words against me.

"How about if I take advantage of you?" I know my bold words aren't something I would say sober, but it feels marvelous to be so free of my typical inhibitions.

He tips his head back and laughs at my outrageous suggestion. "I would love that, but somehow, I think it would still be *me* taking advantage of the situation."

"What situation?" I pout my lips out, hoping it looks cute and not pathetic. "You drank just as much as I did."

Nodding, Shay confirms. "I did, yet it seems to be having more of an effect on you than it is me."

Giving it one last try, I say, "Come inside with me. Please."

I am both shocked and thrilled when Shay says

"Okay," and follows me over the threshold into his tiny, barren room.

19

I wake up feeling warm and safe. Strong arms are locked around me, protecting me. A delightful masculine and piney smell greets my nose. I take a deep breath, savoring the moment, wanting it to last as long as possible.

When my eyes flutter open, vague memories start to return. My head is resting on Shay's chest as it rises and falls with his even breathing. Broad beams of sunlight are streaking in through the curtains.

Bolting upright, I ask, "What time is it?"

I'm stunned when Shay answers, "10:45 or so." I have never slept this late in my entire life… not even when I had the flu.

My shock over the late hour is nothing compared to the bass drum pounding in my head. I lift my palm up to press against my temple.

"I thought you might have a headache, so I texted one of my coworkers to request medicine and water. It should be right outside the door," he tells me as he stands to retrieve it.

Sure enough, he returns to the bed with bottles of aspirin and water. Tapping two pills out he hands them to me before opening the water bottle. I toss back the pills and wash them down before asking, "Room service delivers headache relievers?"

"For me, they do," he gives me a cocky grin that makes me wonder who he flirts with on the delivery staff to get such customized service.

I don't have long to ponder that worrisome thought because my eyes are drawn down to the giant dark colored circle on Shay's gray tee shirt. I'm horrified when I realize that I have drooled on him in my sleep.

His eyes follow the direction of mine. "Oh, that, yeah... You drool in your sleep, but it's nothing compared to the snoring."

"What?!? I don't snore." I snap, feeling annoyed that he's picking on me like this.

"Yes, you do," he confirms, nodding his head. "I wish I could say it's cute little puffs of air, but it's actually a scary, frog-croaking sort of sound that comes from deep in your throat."

My eyes widen as I look at him, hoping for some sign that he is just teasing me, but there isn't a hint of amusement in his expression. My throat feels parched like it's filled with cotton balls as I take another sip of water from the bottle and try to comprehend what has happened here.

Feeling fuzzy on the details after we returned to the room, I know that I'm going to have to ask

Shay the most humiliating question of my entire life. "Did we... umm... you know?"

"Have sex?" He offers helpfully.

At my mortified nod, he answers, "Believe me... If we had, you would remember."

I narrow my gaze into a steely glare. "Aren't you late for work?" Calling what he does out on the beach 'work' is a bit of a stretch, but I am ready for him to leave.

He shrugs his shoulders, says "I guess I am a little late," and saunters out of the room, closing the door quietly behind him.

I blow the sweaty hair back off my face, certain that I would indeed remember being intimate with that sexy hunk of manhood.

When I get up and walk to the bathroom, I catch a glimpse of my hung-over reflection. My horrified, garbled groan at the crazy-haired, deathly-pale, raccoon-eyed woman with fuzzy teeth staring at the mirror in front of me sends me straight back to bed.

I can't believe Shay saw me looking and smelling like this. I'll never be able to face him again.

The sudden, frantic knock at my door brings me out of my worry fest. For a moment, I think the pounding has returned inside my head, but it pauses for a moment and resumes with even more urgency.

"Hold your horses. I'm coming," I say to the closed door as I stand up and make my way over to answer it.

I had been expecting to see a frazzled Jamie or the nervous bride-to-be on the other side of the door, so I am stunned to discover my normally mellow friend, Roxy.

Her beautiful eyes are wide open as her words rush out in a flurry. "Andrew's family's flights are delayed because of the weather. The flowers for Ruthie's bouquet and the trellis arrived, but they sat out in the sun on the dock too long and are all wilted. The dress shipment says it has been delivered, but no one has seen it. And Grandmother Rose is driving everyone crazy."

This is the first time I have ever seen my beautiful friend so flustered. I reach out to take her hand and bring her inside my tiny room. "It's okay… Take a deep breath. We'll deal with everything one issue at a time."

My calming words seem to work because she plops down on the bed and runs her fingers through her long, dark, and glossy hair. Noticing her surroundings for the first time, she wrinkles her pert nose. "This is your room?"

I smile, knowing my accommodations aren't nearly as luxurious as the resort's guest suites. "Shay loaned me his employee housing, and he's staying on his boat. Remember?"

It dawns on me then that he technically stayed here with me last night, but I'm certain that was a one-time deal. After seeing my morning-after look, without the benefit of the nighttime fun, I'm sure the last thing he wants is to spend any more time with me.

"Hmm," Roxy says noncommittally, but I know her well enough to see that the wheels of her mind are turning with possibilities.

Knowing I need to shut that down before she

and Ruthie devise any crazy matchmaking plans, I say, "He's sweet and sexy," at her raised brows, I quickly add, "But he's not right for me. He has no ambition or career goals."

Roxy's nodding, but I can tell she isn't convinced. "He sits on the beach renting beach toys all day, for Pete's sake."

"Sounds like a great life," Roxy weighs in before her perfectly arched brows tug together. "Hey! What's wrong with working on the beach to make a living? I paint and sell my artwork from a beach hut very similar to Shay's. It's a much more fulfilling career for me than accounting was."

I don't want Roxy to think I look down on her career choice. "Selling artwork that you have created is way different than renting boogie boards or Sea-Doos by the hour."

Roxy shrugs her shoulders. "Not really," she tells me, but she doesn't sound perturbed.

Wanting to move off this topic, I say, "Let me get cleaned up, and we'll dive into resolving these wedding issues."

Nodding and standing to leave, Roxy says, "Sounds good." Pausing before she reaches the door, she turns back to look over her shoulder at me. "I'm glad to have you back in our family, Lizzie."

Smiling at her, I say honestly, "I'm thrilled to be welcomed back into your family. I was miserable without you."

"Same." I see the shift in Roxy's expression to an ornery one that mirrors the perpetual gleam in Baggy's gaze. "Don't rule Shay out as a beach bum just yet. You might be surprised how magical things can get when you loosen up a little."

I'm amazed how much my formerly uptight friend has changed since marrying Kai. When she holds her thumb and pinkie up over her shoulder in a classic shaka sign, I can't help but laugh.

"Yeah, I'm not exactly a 'hang loose' type of lady," I call out to her back, but she is already closing the door behind her. Once she's gone, I can't help but wonder if I would look as happy as she does, if I could manage to cut loose a little bit.

20

*O*nce I'm clean and presentable, I head out to find the others. Both Ruthie and Roxy seem frazzled, so I slide into my comfortable role of efficient taskmaster. I'm careful not to be too bossy, but I give everyone chores to follow-up on from my master list.

Grandmother Rose is the only one I don't assign with a wedding prep task. She seems content to glare down her nose at the rest of us, and I don't want to deal with her holier-than-thou attitude.

Jamie is also carrying a clipboard, and she seems to be actively avoiding me. I can't help but wonder if her list of tasks is filled with items to throw the wedding off-kilter. Deciding that if that is the case, she is only complying with the sabotage to keep her job, I resolve to deal with any problems that arise calmly and rationally.

The humid air already has me sweating, and I can feel my curls growing exponentially, but I am not here to look good. I am here to make sure Ruthie's wedding goes off without a hitch.

I am using my headset to talk to a travel agent to try to reroute Andrew's family to get them here in time for tomorrow's wedding. Only a few flights haven't been cancelled due to the impending storm, but I am determined to score them seats.

"There must be people who have changed their minds about coming here after watching the weather reports," I say to the woman on the other end of the phone.

"Actually, there aren't any seats available on the direct flight from Atlanta." I can hear her keyboard clacking in the background.

"Then find them a flight from another airport, and we'll figure out how to get them there."

More keyboard tapping ensues. "I can get three of them on a flight from New York and the other two on one from Boston, but it's going to be expensive."

"Book it!" I tell her, hoping that the show is going to foot the bill.

As I'm finalizing the details for the Starks' travel with her, a line begins to form of people waiting to speak with me. While the woman has me on hold as she books the needed travel arrangements, I make my way through the line.

After helping Caroline finalize the reception dinner menu, assisting Roxy with the bumbled flower order, choosing the right color for the tuxedo ties and cummerbunds, and helping Andrew with the word choice for his vows, I

116

realize that Shay has been waiting patiently at the end of the line.

His hands are behind his back as he takes the final steps towards me. "Are you able to stop for some lunch?"

"I don't have time." I use my hand to indicate the unending to-do list on my clipboard.

"Thought you might say that." He smiles and brings a wrapped sandwich and chips out from behind his back. After handing me the food, he leans down to kiss my cheek and says, "You need to eat."

"I will," I promise him as I gladly accept his generous and thoughtful offering. "Yes, I'm here," I say into my phone when the travel agent comes back from having me on hold. I mouth the words 'thank you' to Shay. He nods and heads back towards the beach.

I smile to myself as I watch him go. Taking a bite of the chicken salad sandwich, I realize that I'm really going to miss having someone who worries so much about making sure my needs are taken care of.

My thoughts are interrupted when Ruthie runs up to me. "Baggy wants to leave the hospital. She says if someone doesn't come get her, she's going to steal a car and drive herself."

I can't stop the chuckle over Baggy's typical spunk. Once that woman gets something into her head, there is no changing her mind.

Ruthie looks really worried, so I place a comforting hand on her forearm. "Don't worry about it. I'll make sure she has a ride."

Even though Ruthie nods, I still see the worry

lines between her brows. "You are supposed to be relaxing. Don't worry about a thing," I assure her. "I've got this."

My voice sounds more confident than I feel. So far, I have been able to adeptly handle any bump that has come along that might ruin Ruthie's big day. I feel confident that I can handle anything the producers try to throw our way. My only concern is what Mother Nature might be planning to hurl at us.

21

I hear Baggy before I see her. "What in the ever-lovin' cock-a-doodle-doo do you mean, telling me that a strawberry daiquiri isn't healthy? I need to get my daily serving of fruit, you know."

Caroline looks exasperated as she tries to explain to her mother that she isn't supposed to drink alcohol with her new medications.

Baggy, who is dressed from head to toe in Adidas athletic gear, makes a scoffing sound in her throat. "They just put those warnings on there to scare people. No one takes them seriously."

"Actually, they do," I jump in, unwilling to let Baggy take any unnecessary risks with her health. Turning to the bartender, I say, "Do you have any more of that delicious mango juice?"

The pretty woman nods, already pouring the bright liquid from a pitcher for Baggy. "There," I tell Baggy, when the glass is presented to her. "You can get your fruit serving with some fresh, chilled juice."

Baggy grumbles, but accepts the glass and takes a tentative sip. I can't help but smile when I see her bluish-silver curls poking out from under her Adidas baseball cap, which she is wearing backwards.

Deciding that I can use a little pick-me-up, I request a Coke. When the bartender gives me the fizzing glass, Baggy sounds like a toddler as she whines. "Why do you get that, and I'm stuck with healthy juice?"

"I need the caffeine." I say to justify my rare cola indulgence.

"You practically bleed caffeine," Baggy accuses me.

I can't deny the truth in her statement, even as I chuckle over her odd observation. I do drink a lot of hot tea, but it seems too sticky outside to indulge in a hot beverage now. The first sip of the ice cold Coke burns down my throat and perfectly hits the spot. I practically groan over how good it tastes.

Baggy is glaring at me. "I want a Coke," she grouches at the bartender, sticking her lip out in full pout mode.

Caroline jumps in to tell her mother that she can have one after she finishes her juice. The entire exchange reminds me of negotiating with a toddler, but I wisely opt not to point that out.

I think we are lucky when Baggy's attention is drawn away, until I see the direction her glare is turned. "What is *she* doing here?" Baggy hisses, with her voice filled with venom.

"She's Ruthie's grandmother, too." Caroline reminds her mother.

"Hardly," Baggy scoffs. "Only if you consider judging and reprimanding to be the job requirements of being a grandmother."

Grandmother Rose's harsh gaze has zeroed in on Baggy, and the woman makes a beeline in our direction. Once she has joined us near the bar, the two older women openly glare at each other.

"Baggy." Grandmother Rose spits the name out as if she has just discovered a coating of slime on her tongue.

"Grandma Petunia." I can't contain my snort over Baggy's immature, obviously intentional bumbling of the other woman's name.

When Grandmother Rose's steely gaze darts to me, I suck in a breath and immediately quiet down. Even though I'm now a grown woman, I still feel intimidated by her constant judgment. It's obvious by her sneer that she finds me to be utterly lacking in social graces.

Some color is returning to Baggy's pallid face, which makes me wonder if this ancient rivalry might actually be good for her health. Focusing on besting Grandmother Rose is obviously one of Baggy's favorite activities.

I look between the two women. Shriveled, feisty Baggy is the opposite of sleek, sophisticated Grandmother Rose in every way––both physically and emotionally. While Grandmother Rose is no stranger to plastic surgery to tighten and firm, Baggy wears her wrinkles and sags like proud battle scars. Baggy's old-fashioned, set pin curls are so unlike Grandmother Rose's smooth, sleek, and pure-white bob.

Even their fashion choices are at opposite ends of the spectrum. I've never seen Grandmother Rose wearing anything but a sophisticated suit and expensive heels. Baggy dresses more for comfort––although today's oversized athletic wear takes that to the extreme.

Once their stare-down reaches the point of discomfort for all of us, Baggy lifts her chin, turns to her daughter and says, "I don't think there is enough chocolate or middle fingers on this entire island to get me through the rest of this weekend with that woman."

Grandmother Rose's mouth falls open in shock over Baggy's brash statement, but we are saved from her retort by the arrival of a slender, handsome-as-sin man.

"Well, if it isn't the most drop-dead gorgeous, outrageously bold, and wonderful woman on this––or any––island." The man stoops to give Baggy a warm hug.

"Syd!" Baggy practically squeals as she jumps and throws her arms around his neck. "Are you here to make me even more beautiful?"

"As if that were even possible." He flirts with her, and it suddenly dawns on me that this man is Ruthie's stylist and confidant from the previous show she was on, *Cruising for Love.*

Having heard enough of Syd's flirtation with Baggy, Grandmother Rose huffs before storming off.

"What's her problem?" Syd asks.

"Oh, you haven't had the displeasure of

meeting Grandmother Rose?" Baggy flutters her lashes up at Syd. "She's the girls' other grandma, and she's the exact opposite of me in every way."

Syd smiles down at the tiny woman. "Well, you're utterly marvelous in every way, so what does that make her?"

"A pain in the ass-anine." Baggy quickly amends her last word, in an attempt to maintain her vow to stop cussing.

Unaware of Baggy's new resolution, but accustomed to her odd comments, Syd nods and chuckles. "Any pain in your ass-anine is also a pain in mine."

Baggy beams up at him, obviously thrilled to have him openly take her side. After quickly introducing Syd to Caroline and me, Baggy says, "Now grab your giant train case full of makeup tools because we have some serious work for you to do."

With that, the tiny woman sets off, dragging the six-foot-tall cackling stylist in her wake.

22

I'm starting to feel like I just might have this wedding under control. Problems arise left and right throughout the day, but I calmly and efficiently handle them… like a boss.

When dusk falls, we walk through the rehearsal, and I begin to realize this entire event could easily be considered a giant fiasco by an outside observer. I just hope the show's editors will be kind when they put it all together.

The pastor, who is performing tomorrow's ceremony, has been delayed, so I stand in and read her part.

Andrew's nephew is supposed to be the ring bearer, but their family's flights are still delayed, so Baggy pretends to play that part. She crawls around on her knees, despite the fact that her diminutive height is practically that of a child's, even when she's standing. She manages to drop the rings in the sand, so we spend at least five minutes searching for them.

Eventually, Jamie comes forward and admits the rings were fake stand-ins and that we should just continue with the rehearsal.

"Fakes?!?" Baggy splutters, obviously outraged. "You didn't trust me with the real rings?" No one dares to point out that they were obviously right not to entrust her with the expensive versions.

We try to resume our practice session, but the wind kicks up and knocks the trellis archway down. Andrew is so surprised by the fracas that he allows the wind to steal the paper from his hand. "My vows!" he yells, chasing after the tiny paper.

His groomsmen and stand-ins follow suit. They all race after the paper, but no one catches it before it blows into the ocean. When Andrew returns to the toppled trellis where we are trying to walk-through the ceremony, his eyes are wide with panic. "I couldn't catch them."

"You remember them, right?" Ruthie tries to smile at him, but it is a wobbly gesture.

Andrew looks at me, silently pleading with me to help him out. Nodding, I answer for him. "Sure, we remember them."

"We?!?" Ruthie looks rather taken aback as she glares in my direction. "You saw his wedding vows?"

"I just helped him with his word choice in a couple of areas," I assure her, knowing she would not appreciate hearing that I had practically written them by myself. Andrew had been completely on board with the sentiment. He just hadn't been sure how to express his feelings.

Ruthie nods, accepting my explanation, but her brow is still furrowed with a hint of annoyance.

Deciding we need to jump back into our practice run before she has time to stew about this any more, I ask once more for everyone's attention.

Almost as soon as things are quieting down, an alarmed scream pierces the air. My eyes dart to Baggy, but she is standing on the sidelines, looking as startled as everyone else. When I follow her stunned gaze, the sight that greets me makes my stomach lurch up to my throat.

Just behind Ruthie's shoulder, her matron-of-honor and only sister, Roxy, has crumpled to the ground.

I lunge forward to check on my best friend in the entire world. My heart races as I check her vitals. Almost as quickly as she lost consciousness, Roxy revives.

Her eyelashes flutter open, and she awakens confused about what happened. I have my arms around her as I tell her that she passed out. Looking up at the gathered crowd, I ask, "Has anyone called an ambulance?"

"No, that's not necessary," Roxy declares vehemently.

Just as stubbornly, I tell her, "You fainted. You need to be checked out by a medical professional."

She's shaking her head at me. "I haven't eaten much today. I probably just overheated."

Just as I'm getting ready to point out that she's been living in Hawaii for months, so she should be used to the heat, a deep voice interrupts. "I'll take care of her."

A huge man with a rich, russet-colored skin tone and shiny black hair emerges from the crowd. From the way his worried eyes frantically search Roxy's face for any sign of how she'd doing, I assume that the newcomer is her husband.

Confirming my suspicion, Roxy's face lights up when she sees him. "Kai," she breathes his name out in a relieved sigh. "I'm okay," she promises him before adding, "Just get me out of here."

Without a moment's hesitation, he bends down and scoops her up as if she is light as a feather. Roxy is slender, but tall. His wide shoulders make carrying her look easy.

"She needs medical attention." I call out to his already retreating back.

"I'll be fine." Roxy calls out over his shoulder before adding confidently, "Kai will take care of me."

With that, the two of them disappear up the trail towards the resort. I am left stunned by the entire chain of events.

Even though it is obvious that Kai's top concern is her well-being, I can't believe that Roxy is choosing to ignore her fainting spell. More than that, though, I want someone in my life to swoop in like a savior and whisk me away like that.

Unbidden, a mental image of Shay's broad shoulders forces its way into my brain. He is certainly strong enough to pick me up like that. I have to force the grin off my face as I wonder what he would do with me once he carried me to safety. My guess is that he would give me a night I would never forget.

The only problem with my entire imagined scenario is that I don't think there is any way that one night of passion in his arms would be nearly enough.

$\mathcal{W}$e quickly run through the remainder of the ceremony and head over to the restaurant for the rehearsal dinner meal. I realize as soon as I cut into the pink center of my chicken that the meat is under-cooked. I make a quick, loud announcement to the group not to eat it, and the plates are quickly whisked back to the kitchen.

Just as I'm beginning to think that I can resolve any problems that might arise––producer-created or natural––it's time to watch the pre-wedding show that will completely deflate my sails.

With the exceptions of Roxy and Kai, our entire group gathers around the big-screen televi-sion in the lobby to watch the show as it streams live to the entire world via the magic of the internet.

I am featured much more frequently and prominently in the opening sequence than I would prefer. It quickly dawns on me that the large cameras being toted around by cameramen aren't the only cameras in use. Hidden cameras evidently record our every move, with the hopeful exception of our bathroom time.

When my conversation with Jamie––that we both thought was private––is broadcast for all to see, our eyes dart to each other.

I hate the sound of my own voice, when I hear the recording of it say about Shay, "I think I might want to have an island romance with him."

Unwilling to face him, I glue my horrified gaze to the television screen, until I hear myself snapping, "Back off––he's mine!" Even though I know the words had been said to Jamie in complete jest, hearing them out of context on the show makes them sound incredibly catty.

By the time it happens, I'm not overly surprised that they have invaded our privacy like this, but my eyes still dart back to Jamie's to gauge her reaction. When I hear my voice share her secret, I feel terrible as the red flush creeps up her cheeks. "You have your own crush. How are things with T.J., anyway?"

The show pauses for a commercial break. Covering her mouth with her hand, Jamie gets up and runs out of the room, obviously humiliated. My first instinct is to run after her, but Ruthie's accusation stops me. "Somehow you've managed to make *my* wedding show all about you."

I'm stunned that she would think this is how I wanted things to go. I hate being the center of attention and would be thrilled to let her have the spotlight. *She must remember this about me, right?* If the way she is glaring at me is any indication, she does not remember this at all.

The show resumes, and the sick feeling that was lightly bubbling deep in my belly turns into a full-fledged erupting volcano. If I didn't know any better, I'd think that I had actually ingested some of the undercooked chicken at dinner.

Forcing my sour stomach down, I watch in stunned disgust as I'm portrayed as the bitchy taskmaster star of Ruthie's pre-wedding show. Glancing over at Ruthie, I see her pinched expression and arms crossed firmly over her chest. This show honestly couldn't be going any worse for my fragile relationship with her.

When I chance a tentative look in Shay's direction, I'm surprised to see him gazing back at me as if I am the only woman in the world. His adoring look feels phenomenal, but I stubbornly try to tamp down the sudden stuttering of my heartbeat. It would be so easy to forget my troubles for a bit in Shay's bed, but I know that particular path will only lead me to heartbreak.

All of the other women on the show somehow look sleek and fabulous, despite the heat. I am the only one who looks like an overheated, sweaty, and frazzled mess.

I want to look back at Shay to see his reaction to how awful I look by comparison, but I fear he'll be looking at me with utter disappointment in his eyes. *How could he not? Roxy and Ruthie are beautiful swans, and I am the consummate ugly duckling.*

Even prim Grandmother Rose looks flawless.

Her unsubtle digs at everyone from the groom to the hotel staff do not cast her in a flattering light, but from the way she is beaming at her likeness on the screen, it is obvious that she doesn't see her own negativity.

They save Baggy's medical emergency for the final segment, likely as a ploy to boost the drama and ratings. Baggy shushes us for her big moment as the camera zooms in on her tiny, crumpled body while I perform C.P.R. on her.

"Why didn't anyone straighten out my glasses?" she asks, sounding perturbed that we didn't pause to make her camera-ready before saving her life.

Again, I am portrayed as the strong heroine in the show, while Ruthie plays the part of a minor extra. Her huff of frustration is amplified by the silence in the room as we all watch the crisis with Baggy unfold. Even though we were all there and know what happens next, watching it occur on the screen is stressful.

"I hope I'm going to be okay," Baggy quips, providing the comedic relief we all need in that moment.

Everyone chuckles, except for Ruthie. She is too busy glaring eye darts in my direction. The last thing I need is to be on her shit list so soon after tentatively making amends with her.

Once the show finally comes to an end, everyone claps and stands up to pat each other on the back. I am quickly engulfed by well-wishers, who tell me how great the show made me look. I silently amend their kind words in my own mind. I looked far from great physically. In fact, I looked like a complete hot mess. But the show did make

me look like an organized––if somewhat control-
ling––heroine, which would be flattering, if the
portrayal and abundance of airtime didn't annoy
Ruthie so much.

By the time I am able to slip away from the
crowd without seeming rude, Ruthie has stormed
off in a huff. Deciding the best thing is probably to
let her cool off a bit, I take out my phone to call
and check on Roxy. She doesn't answer, so I head
to the front desk to find out her room number. I
won't be able to sleep tonight, until I know for
sure that she is okay.

The front desk crew is busy with storm preparations. The phones are ringing off the hook and
concerned guests are standing in line to ask if they
should evacuate. With the pre-wedding hubbub, I
had nearly managed to forget about the quickly
approaching storm. Based on everyone's drawn
expressions, it's obvious that the storm is still
barreling in our direction.

I patiently wait in line for my turn. When I
finally reach the front of the line, the harried front
desk clerk gives me a pitiful expression as she
asks, "What can I do for you?" She doesn't even
attempt to smile.

Thinking that I am going to be her easiest
request of the evening, I give her a warm smile.
"I'm just here to get the room number for my
friend, Roxy…"

My eyes widen as I realize that I don't know
what Roxy's new last name is. I hadn't been
invited to her wedding to Kai, for obvious reasons,
and I can't recall ever hearing her married name.

The front desk clerk taps her fingernails lightly

on her keyboard, obviously annoyed by my confusion. Needing to try something, I say Roxy's maiden name, in case she didn't change it when she got married. "Rose."

After some fast clacking on the computer's keys, the woman looks up at me. "We don't have a guest by that name." It's obvious by the way she tries to look around me that she wants me to go away.

I need to check on Roxy's health, so I'm not willing to give up that easily. "Look," I try. "This is my best friend in the entire world, and she passed out tonight. I just want to check if she's okay. She is the sister to the bride for the show that is filming here. Maybe they have a block of rooms that I could go check?"

The woman is no longer even attempting to hide her perturbed expression from me. "Look," she mimics my tone, "If you're really such good friends with her, why hasn't she told you her room number?"

I feel like blustering over her rudeness. Even though it is obvious that she is stressed, she shouldn't be taking it out on me.

Shay swoops in, seemingly from out of nowhere. "Lila," he flashes his white teeth at the frazzled woman.

When I see her grin back at him as her cheeks flush a pretty shade of pink, I feel like gagging. Shay's seemingly effortless charm is already working better than my best friendly inquiry.

"I can vouch for Lizzie. She's an integral part of the show." Forming his brow into a furrowed vee, he adds, "Mmm... You must have missed the airing of it, since you were stuck behind this desk. I'll send you a link to the replay. It's definitely worth watching."

Lila's face visibly brightens at his sympathy and kind offer.

"Now," he continues, taking advantage of her warm gaze by leaning on the high desktop. "I know the show booked a block of rooms. Any chance you could take a quick gander through them to see which one is reserved under Roxy's name?"

The woman is already pulling up the information on her screen. I feel like screaming that she could have done that when I politely asked, but I don't want to stop her from getting the information I need.

"Room 134," she beams at Shay, before turning a much cooler, narrowed gaze in my direction.

"You're the best. Thank you." Shay winks at her, which makes the woman practically titter.

It's all I can do not to roll my eyes at the ridiculous exchange, but he has managed to get the information I need, so I force myself to refrain. Once we are out of earshot from the front desk, I hiss at him, "It must be nice to be so charming that people practically fall over themselves to give you what you want."

I had intended the words to be snarky, but Shay takes them as a compliment. Beaming at me, he asks, "You think I'm charming?"

The question is basically rhetorical, so I don't bother to answer. Instead, I whirl around and head towards Room 134. It doesn't surprise me that he follows me. What does surprise me is that I am glad to sense him behind me. I can tell that my heart is in danger with this flippant, flirtatious man, but my best efforts to protect it don't seem to be working.

hen we reach the door for Roxy's room, I raise my hand to knock on it. She and Kai are still relative newlyweds, but considering her fainting episode earlier, I'm assuming I won't be interrupting a romantic interlude between them.

Kai answers the door, but keeps the opening narrow. "Hi, I'm Roxy's friend, Lizzie." I tell him, inserting extra friendliness into my voice, since my reputation likely precedes me.

His expression remains aloof, and he continues to block the doorway. Undaunted by his chilly reception, I ask, "Is Roxy feeling okay?"

"She's fine." He looks like he might be considering shutting the door in my face, so I rise onto my tiptoes in an attempt to see past him and into the room. His shoulders are broad enough to completely obstruct my view.

Evidently hearing the exchange, Roxy yells out, "I'm fine, Lizzie. Don't worry."

From the tone of her voice, it is obvious that she is still peaked. Her attempt at hiding it fails. "Worrying is what I do," I remind her with a smile, even though she can't see me past her hulking husband.

Kai's face softens slightly before he says, "I'm taking care of her."

Roxy backs him up. "Please go out and have some fun. I'm in good hands." I hear her mumble for Kai's ears, "the best, actually," but I choose to ignore that.

"Can I bring you anything?" I yell past her protective husband.

"I'm good. I'll see you tomorrow." Roxy responds, effectively shutting down my offer of help.

"Okay, bye," I tell her, but Kai is already shutting the door in my face.

When I whirl around to face Shay, who has just witnessed the entire exchange, I don't bother to hide the perturbed look on my face. After walking a few steps away from their door, so I am sure we are out of earshot, I ask him, "Did that seem strange to you? Why wouldn't he let me see her? You don't suppose he's in some way abusive towards her, do you?"

My eyes widen and my heart rate speeds up with each new question that pops into my head and out of my mouth. "If he hurts her, I'll kill him."

Shay holds up his hand in mock surrender. "Whoa! Slow down and back up a little bit."

I turn a fiery glare up towards him. "If Roxy's in danger, I will protect her."

"I have no doubt about that," he tries to appease me. "You are obviously fiercely protective of your friends."

"What's wrong with that?" I ask him, immediately feeling defensive.

"Nothing at all," he confirms. "In fact, it's one of your most endearing qualities."

I want to hear more about what he considers my other 'endearing qualities' to be, but he doesn't expand on it. Instead, he weighs in with his opinion on Roxy's situation.

"Roxy seems madly in love with her husband, and she doesn't strike me as the shrinking violet type. I think if he was hurting her, she would say something."

I nod, silently admitting that he's probably right about that. Unwilling to just let it go, I ask, "But why wouldn't he let me see her? He was purposely blocking the doorway."

"Maybe he was trying to protect her." Shay suggests gently.

"From me?" I practically squawk. "I'm her best friend."

"But how much does he know about your friendship? Most of what he knows about you probably involves her ruined first wedding. Now, don't get me wrong, I'm sure he's grateful that you stopped her from marrying the wrong man, but I think we all know that the way it happened was not ideal."

Shame burns hot on my cheeks as I remember that Shay knows all about my lapse in judgment and betrayal of my best friend's trust. For some reason, it's important to me that he knows that was a one-time mistake, and not at all the way I normally behave.

"The night before Roxy's wedding, I made the biggest blunder of my entire life. I've been paying for it every moment since. I lost my best friend and her family, which is my family-by-choice over that mistake. I've been working since that moment to earn back their trust. I don't deserve their forgiveness, but they are starting to give it to me anyway."

I feel tears burning at the backs of my eyes as I speak, but once I start, I can't seem to stop. "Roxy and her family are the most important people in my life, outside of my own mother. I have to win them back. My life is shit without them."

"You do deserve them in your life, Lizzie." Shay tells me earnestly. His clear gaze is unwavering. "Everyone makes mistakes. You have apologized and paid your penance. They are forgiving you, but you might need to give Kai a little extra time. I get the sense that he is very protective of his wife."

I'm surprised by how intuitive Shay is. He has only known us a short time, but he seems to already have his finger on the pulse of our interactions. "That makes sense," I admit, nodding that he's right.

Sensing the need for a change of subject, Shay says, "It will all work out. But do you know what you need tonight?"

Curious where he is going with this, I respond warily, "What?"

"To relax on the beach with a delicious, frozen alcoholic beverage," he suggests.

Deciding that he might just be right about that, I lock elbows with him and say, "That sounds wonderful."

With that, we set off in search of a bottle of rum.

25

*S*hay and I sit out on the beach, talking and laughing and drinking frozen banana daiquiris. Every time my slushy beverage begins to run low, Shay runs up to the poolside bar to get us refills.

"I like having a bottomless drink," I reveal, grinning up at him when he returns with our third or fourth refills. It dawns on me that I should be concerned that I can't remember exactly how many drinks we have downed, but I am too relaxed and happy to care.

"Thrilled to be of service," Shay tells me before rejoining me on the blanket stretched out on the sand.

We have the entire beach to ourselves. The only signs of life are the bopping reggae music and the murmur of flirtatious laughter wafting over from the outdoor bar.

I look up at the clear sky and am shocked to discover what seems like a million stars twinkling above us. Shay puts an arm around me as we both rest back on the blanket to look at them.

The lulling sound of the ocean's waves rolling into shore, combined with the numbing effects of the rum, make me feel as relaxed as warm putty. "It's so peaceful out here," I murmur barely loud enough to be heard.

Proving that he did hear me, Shay responds sleepily, "This really is the calm before the storm."

We must have dozed off, because the next thing I know, I awaken to large drops of water splashing down onto my face. Bolting upright, I startle Shay awake. The wind has kicked up enough that the lulling ebb and flow of the ocean's waves has morphed into repetitive crashing sounds that beat at the shoreline.

Huge drops of water plop straight down from the sky, pelting us. We quickly stand to find shelter. Shay grabs the blanket from the beach, but when he lifts it, the wild wind catches it and blows sand into our faces.

I cover my eyes with my arm and run towards the room Shay has loaned me. My assumption is that he is following me, but I don't dare risk turning back for fear of more sand blowing into my eyes.

Once I reach the overhang for the employee housing, I turn my face to the side and am pleased to see that Shay is right behind me. Yelling over the howling wind, I ask, "Is this the storm or just a squall moving through?"

"I think this is the beginning edge of the storm," he confirms.

As if Mother Nature has heard his proclamation, a gust of wind blows past us, nearly toppling me. Shay reaches a hand out to steady me. "You better get inside," he warns me.

Nodding I reach into my pocket for the key to his room. Digging around in first one, then the other pocket, my hand comes out empty. My alarmed expression must give me away because Shay asks, "No key?"

"It must have fallen out on the beach," I confirm, even as I'm trying to imagine searching the sand in the dark for it. "Do you happen to have a spare?" I ask, already guessing the answer.

"No," he shakes his head.

My eyes light up with an idea. "The front desk must have one."

I am already turning towards the main building of the resort when I hear Shay making a doubtful sound, "Mnn... They have keys for the guest rooms, but not the employee housing."

At my deflated look, he adds, "Maintenance has a master key, but I hate to wake them up in the middle of the night."

I don't really want to wake anyone up either, but I don't see another option. Lifting my shoulders, I say, "Well, I can't sleep out here."

"No," Shay grins down at me before adding, "But you can sleep on my boat... with me."

Even though the wind is howling around us, I suddenly feel like I can't get enough air into my lungs. "I... You... We can't..."

Even though the liquor flowing through my

veins is making my lips loose, I can't find the words to express my confusion. As much as I would love to spend the night on Shay's boat with him, I know that I would feel guilty about it later. Sleeping with him when I know we have no real chance of having a future together feels wrong, despite how tempting it is to throw caution to the wind and just do it––as one of Baggy's desired corporate sponsors would say.

Shay's mesmerizing blue gaze is peering down at me as if I am the most entertaining person he has ever encountered. He seems to be enjoying watching me squirm. Putting me out of my misery, he holds his hands up with his palms facing me. "I won't touch you. I promise."

I manage to morph my expression into a relieved look, even though that isn't at all what I'm feeling.

Why does he have to be such a gentleman all the time? The wayward thought catches me off guard. Shaking my head, I realize it's no wonder men find women to be so perplexing. I can't even figure out in my own mind what I want. The logical side of me wants to avoid him and protect my heart, but there's a warring faction inside me––I grin as I decide to call her the vixen––who wants nothing more than for him to take me to his bed and make me forget everything but our mutual explosive pleasure and release.

Not wanting to give him any hint about my internal struggle, I say, "I suppose that's my best option, under the unfortunate circumstances."

He looks amused by my unenthusiastic response. "You choose me," he teases me.

"Only because the other options are shit," I remind him, giving his shoulder a good-natured shove to show him I'm teasing.

Furrowing his brow and pretending to truly be concerned, Shay asks me, "Would Baggy approve of you cussing like that?"

"Baggy cusses more than any person I know," I tell him honestly before adding, "This vow of hers not to cuss will never last."

"She seems to be pretty committed to it." He weighs in.

Deciding he's right, I amend my previous statement. "Okay, the other options were shi-poopy."

Shay tips his head back and laughs at my accurate depiction of how Baggy would alter the word when it was already partially out of her mouth. Slinging an arm around me, he guides me towards the marina where his boat is docked.

He steadies me as I climb aboard the ancient, teakwood sailboat. I venture below-decks and discover the tiny bedroom. The bed is narrow–– barely wide enough for the two of us to fit.

"Want to do head-to-toe or under-over?" he asks from right behind me, proving that he indeed intends to be a perfect gentleman tonight.

"Under-over," I answer, trying not to let the sound of my frustrated sigh of disappointment carry over to him.

*P*roving that he is indeed a gentleman, Shay kicks off his flip-flops and plops down on top of the covers. I peel the cool cotton top sheet and light quilt back, kick off my own shoes, and climb into his bed.

We both lie perfectly straight and flat on our backs. I can feel the heat emanating from him, even though we aren't physically touching. The tiny cabin is surprisingly cool, as a fresh, briny sea breeze wafts in through the open windows.

It irks me beyond reason when Shay's breath evens out. He hasn't had any trouble drifting off to sleep, while I can't shut my mind off enough to stop thinking about how close we are or what would happen if I reached out to touch him.

I wonder if he would decline my advance or if he is just keeping his word to not touch me. If I make the first move, it will give him a clear message that I am ready to shift our relationship to a physical one.

When he begins to lightly snore, I let my frustration huff out in a sigh. It doesn't seem fair that I should be wide awake, stressing about when--or even if--we are ever going to act on our desire, while he sleeps peacefully as if he doesn't have a care in the world.

My stress escalates as I wonder if his easy slumber is an indication that he doesn't feel the same magnetic attraction to me as I feel for him. Either being in this close proximity doesn't bother him in the slightest, or he is blessed with the gift of being able to drop off to sleep anywhere and anytime. I have always been jealous of Baggy's ability to do this. If she sits down for more than thirty seconds, she drifts off to sleep.

I guess that's one of the benefits of not having any worries. My busy mind won't shut down long enough to let me drift off into oblivion. Even tonight, when I've had too much to drink and stayed up way past my bedtime, my eyes are wide open as I stew about everything from Ruthie's wedding tomorrow to why the blasted man beside me doesn't want to touch me.

The rain pelting the boat and the wind rocking us back and forth on the water must eventually lull me to sleep because I wake up with a start. Bolting upright in the bed, I wonder what time it is.

I had planned to get up by 5:00 a.m. at the latest, to get started on last minute wedding preparation details. My internal clock tells me that it is already much later than that, so I am most likely already behind on the day's planned activities, even before I start.

Groping around for my cell phone, I push the button to check the time, but am disappointed to see that the blasted device is dead. I look for a charger, but don't see one. Deciding that I'll check the weather before I wake up Shay, I climb the steps to go out on the deck. What I see when my head clears the surface makes a garbled, horrified scream emerge from my throat as I turn to look around in each direction.

"What's wrong?" Shay bolts out of bed and is standing just behind me. I turn and climb back down the steps and stare at him with wide, frightened eyes. Looking truly concerned, Shay asks again, "What is it?"

I point up the stairs, "We… Water everywhere… Storm…" I'm too flustered to spit out the problem, so Shay eases past me to climb the steps to see for himself.

When he rejoins me downstairs, he is as soaked by the pelting rain as I am. He bursts out with laughter, and I have to quell the urge to smack at him. "What are you laughing about? We're lost at sea!" I screech.

He contains his laughter and gives me a soft look. "There's nothing to be afraid of. We're not lost. I'll get us back to shore."

Although he sounds confident in his sailing skills, I still feel doubtful. "Maybe I should call for help. Where is your cell phone?"

"Don't have one," he responds simply, as if this is the most normal thing in the world.

"You don't have a cell phone?" I don't even bother to hide the shock and disdain in my tone.

"No," he says simply. When I continue to gawk

at him, he explains further. "I decided a long time ago that I want to live my life and enjoy the moment. I see too many people come to the beach and fail to appreciate the beauty surrounding them because they are too busy staring at a tiny electronic screen."

There is no denying that he has a point, but I am beginning to feel panicky and more than a little desperate for a way to call for assistance. "I suppose that means you don't have a charger that I can use for my phone, either?"

I already know the answer, but he shakes his head to confirm that my assumption is correct. Snapping my fingers as the idea pops into my head, I say, "You must have a radio on here. We can call the Coast Guard."

He gives me a placating smile, which irritates me to no end. "They are probably plenty busy dealing with real emergencies."

Just as I'm getting ready to shake my finger at him and tell him that he needs to wake up and realize this is an emergency, he continues. "I've sailed through much worse weather than this. I'll get us back to the island."

He sounds so confident that I'm tempted to believe him. When he goes to his closet to retrieve a yellow rain slicker, I ask if he has one for me.

His expression looks surprised, but he offers, "You can stay down here."

"I want to help," I offer, even as I wonder if my lack of sailing skills will make me more of a hindrance than help.

"I'd rather you stayed safely down here," he tries, but my expression must look determined because he tosses a second rain jacket in my direction. "Suit yourself, but you have to follow my directions immediately and precisely."

My initial reaction is to balk at his demanding attitude, but I know that he is the only one who knows how to get us out of this dangerous situation. I zip up the rain jacket, tighten my hood, and nod my agreement that I will comply with his orders.

Even though I'm trying to hide the fact that I'm frightened half to death, my fear must show on my face because Shay pauses to look at me. Lifting his hand to my cheek, he promises earnestly, "I won't let anything happen to you."

Despite how scared I am, I believe him. After nodding with more conviction, I follow him when he heads back up to the deck.

The wind nearly knocks me off my feet, but Shay reaches out a hand to steady me. Leaning in so I can hear, he says, "I'd feel better if you were safely tucked away downstairs. I can handle this alone."

I'm touched that he is so concerned about my safety, but I refuse to let him face this storm without assistance. "I want to help. Just tell me what needs to be done."

Even though we are standing close together, we have to yell to be heard over the wind. Rain pelts my face as I squint up at him.

Suddenly feeling hopeful, I ask, "Does this thing have an engine? Can we just motor into shore?"

"It does have a motor that I've been meaning to fix, but I haven't gotten around to it."

I feel like screaming at him over his lackadaisical attitude, but I know this isn't the time or the place for that.

Suddenly a huge problem dawns on me. My facial expression must convey my concern because Shay asks, "What is it?"

I'm wishing we'd had this conversation below decks where it is dry, but I want to hear his answer too much to wait. "The wind blew us out here."

"It did," he confirms, obviously not understanding why I'm so worried.

"Well then, isn't it blowing in the wrong direction to get us back to the island?"

He has the audacity to grin at me, which totally irks me, since I'm super-stressed about making it back in time for Ruthie's wedding.

"Your lack of faith in my sailing abilities is somewhat offensive," he teases me before explaining. "We are going to travel windward by zigzagging back and forth to reach our target. It's called tacking."

He seems to know what he's talking about, so I decide I really don't have another alternative except to trust him. "Tell me what to do to help."

With that, he begins barking orders that I follow to the best of my abilities. We work together tirelessly to fight against all that Mother Nature is kicking up in our way.

A couple of times, we crash so hard into massive waves that I have to grab ahold of the boat to keep from being swept over the side. Shay keeps a close eye on me, but I wonder what he would do if I fall overboard. If he abandoned ship, we would both be doomed for sure. Trying to force that possibility out of my head, I work to follow his directions.

When I catch a glimpse of land in the gray horizon, I am so relieved that I fear I might burst into tears. My arms and legs are weary with over-exertion, and I am drenched from head to toe, but I am safe.

I point to the hazy mass and Shay nods confidently as if he knows exactly where we are. It doesn't seem possible that he can have any idea of our location, considering the blasting storm that has been carrying our tiny watercraft across the angry ocean.

It dawns on me that we are probably approaching a different island, but at this point, I am so happy to be approaching landfall, I don't even care. I'll figure out another way to return to Antigua for the wedding––preferably not by boat. In fact, I may never step foot on another boat again.

When we approach the shore, I am stunned to recognize our resort. A couple of dockworkers run out to help Shay secure the boat. Once it is tied off, I gladly step onto the dock. I'm so incredibly grateful to be back on solid ground, it is tempting to bend down and kiss the wooden walkway.

I manage to refrain from that, but when Shay steps off the boat, I throw myself into his arms. "You saved us."

"You doubted me?" He seems taken aback that I wasn't confident in his sailing skills against an angry storm.

"Yeah," I admit, and I hear the dockworkers snicker behind us before jogging back towards the shelter of the marina.

Knowing that I must look like a drowned rat and not caring, I tip my heels up and plant a kiss right on Shay's surprised lips. It only takes a moment for him to react. He pulls me into his strong embrace and presses his lips into mine.

The dark gray sky is pelting rain down on us, the wind is howling around us, and we are making out like our life depends on it.

Eventually, Shay pulls back and kisses me lightly on the end of my wet nose. "We need to get you dried off before you catch a cold."

It seems strange to even think about a cold in the steamy heat of the storm. Sucking in a breath as the reality beyond my survival comes crashing back into my mind, I say, "I have to go," before turning and running up the dock.

27

"*Y*ou're okay." The relief is obvious in Roxy's voice as she sees me entering the bridal suite.

"I'm fine," I promise, confident that I don't look it. "You're the one I'm worried about. Are you okay?"

"I am now," Roxy says. "I've been worried to death about you," she accuses as she pulls me into a hug.

Not wanting to muss her already gorgeous makeup and hair, I say, "I'm a mess."

"I don't care," Roxy insists, wrapping her arms around me.

Ruthie runs up to wiggle her way into our hug. "What happened? You scared us half to death."

Her tone doesn't sound accusatory. I'm touched that, despite being mad about the show's focus on me, she is still this concerned about my wellbeing. "I'm fine," I promise, before adding, "Thanks to Shay."

Both girls' eyebrows shoot up with interest, but before they can ask me any questions, Baggy squeezes into our three-way hug and pops up in the middle. "Are we having a gosh durn wedding today, or what?"

"Absolutely!" I confirm just as Syd emerges from a dressing room.

Jamie walks out just behind him. "Whoa!" I say as I pull back from the group hug to get a good look at her. Her glasses have been replaced by contacts, but this is more than a Clark Kent to Superman transformation. Her subtle makeup makes her features pop, and her long hair falls in soft waves past her shoulders, replacing the tight ponytail she normally sports. Her silk dress hugs her curves, accentuating them, rather than hiding them like her normal bulky wardrobe does.

"You look gorgeous," I rave honestly. The others quickly follow suit, agreeing with my assessment.

Syd bugs his eyes out in my direction. "What is happening here?" he slowly walks in a complete circle around me. "Oh honey, we have our work cut out for us."

"What… You don't like the drowned rat look?" I grin at the others.

Unable to joke about my drenched state, Syd says seriously. "No." All business, he adds, "You go take a shower. I'll be ready to make you fabulous as soon as you're clean and dry."

I have no doubt that he will do just that, so I gladly head to the suite's bathroom to comply with his request. When I emerge from the shower, I am thrilled to find that someone has left a soft, fluffy robe on the sink for me.

As soon as I come out of the bathroom, Syd whisks me into his dressing room to beautify me. He turns me away from the mirror while he works, so I close my eyes and enjoy the undivided attention. When he whirls my chair around so I can see the lighted mirror, I'm delighted to find that he has worked absolute magic on my normally average features. My eyes are expertly lined, my lips shimmer, and my hair is miraculously frizz-free––for the first time since arriving on this island. Instead, it curls gently around my face.

"Wow, can I take you with me everywhere?" I practically gasp at the makeover he has performed on me.

"For a small fee," he quips, smiling.

The ladies fawn appropriately over my new look when I rejoin them in the suite. As much as I enjoy their compliments, I know we are running behind. Quickly sliding back into my planning role, I begin asking questions and barking orders to get this wedding back on track.

I refuse to let a tropical storm, ratings-seeking producers, or anything else ruin Ruthie's big day. *I've got this under control. I hope...*

28

*M*y confidence in my problem-solving abilities might have been a little bit premature. The constant bombardment of new issues is beginning to grate on my already-frazzled nerves. I fear that I might sweat through the gorgeous gown Syd selected for me to wear from his rolling rack of to-die-for dresses.

I have set up shop in the resort's small business center, and I am trying to deal with new snags one at a time, even though they are arriving in droves. From flower delivery snafus to lost wedding bands and bickering grandmothers, I forge through each new problem with as much dignity and calmness as I can muster.

When Jamie runs in and announces that the white tent we scrambled to set up has blown away, I feel like crying. Instead, I take a deep breath before asking her, "Can we get it set back up with more reinforcements?"

She's already shaking her head before I get the

question fully out of my mouth. "It won't stay. The wind is too strong. Besides, I think the top ripped when it got caught on a piling."

"Great," I mutter sarcastically before asking her, "Is there any way T.J. will let us postpone the wedding until the storm passes through? We just can't deal with all of these weather issues, on top of everything else." I don't bother to point out the vast majority of 'everything else' is likely being orchestrated by the crew––possibly including Jamie––to make the show more dramatic.

"I wish, but they have already announced the timing of the airing of the show. It was already a super-tight timeline for editing, but we need to make sure we are the first to air. The paparazzi are already hiding behind potted plants, hoping to get the first photo of Ruthie in her wedding gown."

This isn't at all what I want to hear, but I remind myself not to shoot the messenger. It isn't really Jamie's fault we are facing these challenging predicaments. Besides, this is what I'm here for... to handle all of these inconveniences, so Ruthie doesn't have to worry.

Not seeing another option, I head up to the bridal suite. The ladies are sipping mimosas from crystal flutes, while wearing silk robes, and getting manicures. It looks like they are having the time of their lives, and I hate to be the bearer of bad news.

Kneeling in front of Ruthie, I look up into her eyes and say, "It's starting to look like we need to move the ceremony inside. This tropical storm is stronger than we thought. The winds just blew the wedding tent away."

She blinks back at me blankly as if not quite

comprehending what I'm telling her. Deciding I better elaborate, I say, "I'm sorry, sweetie. I know you wanted a beachside wedding, but I just don't think it's going to be possible with the show's time crunch."

The sight of the giant tears welling that Ruthie is valiantly trying to hold back from falling makes me feel like screaming. She puts on a brave face before nodding and croaking out the word, "Okay."

The old Ruthie I know would have immediately turned into Bridezilla and pitched a fit about not having the wedding of her dreams. She would have thrown a shoe at the wall and exclaimed that since she was being forced to have her ceremony inside, she might as well have stayed home and had her wedding at our local Comfort Inn.

I know how to deal with that spoiled, bratty version of Ruthie. I would sternly tell her to calm down and to appreciate how fortunate she is, while gently reminding her that things won't always go perfectly and that the most important thing is that she is getting to marry the love of her life today.

Ruthie's new mature and stoic personality is throwing me for a loop, though. I'm not at all sure how to handle it. Yelling at her isn't an option, and she's already being brave and gracious. This strong, kindhearted bride deserves to have the wedding of her dreams, and I hate it that I'm not able to make it happen for her.

Rather than focusing on calming an irate Ruthie down, I find that I'm the one who needs to blow off some steam. I bolt out of the room––forgetting my rain slicker––and run outside.

It dawns on me as the rain pelts my face and the wind whips my dampening hair that I am making a mess of Syd's hard work and the lovely gown he procured for me, but I need to get away for a bit. I'm not overly surprised to find that the only person I want to see right now is Shay.

When I check his boat, I'm disappointed to find that he isn't there. I know he isn't out on the beach in this storm, so I head up to the resort's main building in the hopes of finding him.

Instead, I find Baggy and Grandmother Rose in a stand-off. They are both beautifully coiffed for the wedding, and they are practically gritting their teeth at each other. Grandmother Rose towers over Baggy as she says, "Over my dead body."

"That can be arranged," Baggy fires back, jabbing a gnarled finger into the startled woman's sternum, proving that she isn't in the least bit intimidated by the other woman's height.

Grandmother Rose gulps in half the air in the room as if she has never been so offended.

"What's going on?" I ask, feeling exasperated by their nonstop bickering.

"Grandma Carnation wants to sit in *my* spot," Baggy tattles and simultaneously works in a dig, never taking her eyes off the other woman.

I hear the moment Grandmother Rose turns to look at me because she gasps in another horrified breath. Even though I don't make eye contact with her, I can feel her icy blue gaze traveling up and down my soggy form. Although she's obviously appalled by how I look, she isn't able to let Baggy have the last word. "It isn't *your* spot. It's *mine*," she hisses.

Baggy turns to me for backup, but instead lifts a hand to her mouth. "Oh, you're gonna be in trouble when Syd sees you." She drags out the word 'trouble' like we're in grade school.

"I'll deal with him," I tell her confidently, even as I wonder if the makeup artist will be furious with me.

Making a snap decision that I hope doesn't cause even more problems, I say to Grandmother Rose, "You can have the seat."

Baggy's fiery gaze beams angry lasers in my direction. I hold out an arm to stop her as the tiny spitfire tries to stomp on my foot. "Baggy! I have a better spot for you," I yell out in my defense.

She pauses with her foot in the air, her curiosity obviously piqued. "Better?"

"Yes, better." I confirm.

She's still holding her foot aloft, waiting to see if my plan is worthy of her letting me off the hook from her swift kick to my shin. She warily asks me, "How is it better than where *she's* sitting?" She jerks her head in the direction of the other woman, even though it's obvious whom she is talking about.

"Because you'll have a special role in the wedding ceremony," I promise her even as I silently pray that I'm not overstepping my bounds with Ruthie.

Her face lights up at this news. "Oh, my." she fluffs her silvery-blue curls. Tipping up to look at Grandmother Rose, while still managing to appear as if she is looking down at her, she adds, "I guess I don't need a regular old seat when I have a *special role* in the ceremony."

"She's just making up something to keep you quiet, you silly old bat." Grandmother Rose proves that she's the queen of glaring down at someone by showing off her mastery of the skill.

Baggy's mouth gapes open as her gaze darts to me. I shake my head to let her know that isn't true, but she isn't appeased. "Take that back," she shouts up at Grandmother Rose.

"Make me!" Grandmother Rose's eyes fire long-held hatred in Baggy's direction as she moves to shove past the smaller woman.

Never one to back down from a challenge, no matter how out-gunned she is, tiny Baggy seizes the opportunity to push the much larger woman. She catches the tall, normally graceful woman mid-step, causing her to lose her balance.

I watch as the scene unfolds in slow motion before my horrified eyes. Grandmother Rose's arms windmill as she tries to catch her balance. The resort's pastry chef chooses that inopportune moment to wheel the cart with the massive, intricately decorated, four-tiered wedding cake out.

Sure enough, Grandmother Rose smashes into the masterpiece, crushing it beyond recognition. Seeing the prissy woman so mussed with icing in her hair and smudges on her face would have been funny, if it hadn't caused the devastation of the wedding cake.

The temperamental pastry chef begins cursing in a language that I'm guessing is German, based on all the angry, guttural 'ichs' and 'achs' spewing out of her mouth. She tosses down her tall, white hat and storms out.

I hold out my hand to help Grandmother Rose stand up. The haughty woman chooses instead to get up without my assistance. When I ask if she's okay, she looks down at her soiled dress and lets out an exaggerated growl before leaving in an obvious snit.

Baggy looks pleased with herself.

Quickly assessing the situation and realizing the cake is beyond repair, I say to her, "Come on, you tiny troublemaker. We have a cake to bake."

$\mathcal{W}$e secure the use of the restaurant's kitchen and get to work. Baggy is the one who taught me how to bake, so we flow together seamlessly in the kitchen.

Before long, she is covered practically from head-to-toe in flour. I'm sure that I don't look much better.

She swipes her hand across her cheek, leaving a trail of icing in its wake. "It might not look pretty, but it sure is going to taste good."

I nod, acknowledging the truth in her statement. No one I know can bake a cake as moist and delicious as Baggy can. It's one of her only traditional grandma traits. Of course, the messy kitchen looks like a five-year-old has been given free rein by the time we're done, but I know the results will taste marvelous.

Once we cool the cake's layers, we begin frosting them. The resulting cake is lopsided and not nearly as perfect as the one that was ruined, but it was baked with love. My guess is that Ruthie will like it far more than she would have that sterile, perfect one––even if it doesn't look as camera-ready.

Feeling proud of ourselves, Baggy and I lean back on the counter to admire our creation. Just as I am getting ready to suggest we go get cleaned up for the ceremony, Shay bursts into the kitchen.

"They said I'd find you here," he tells me. I can tell by his uncharacteristically rushed tone that something is terribly wrong. I stay quiet, waiting for him to spill it. "Ruthie needs you. Her dress doesn't fit."

Of all the things I had imagined going wrong, this was far worse. I ordered a back-up dress, but the storm delayed the islands deliveries, and it hasn't yet arrived. "We have to get her into it," I mutter almost to myself, already jogging towards the kitchen's door.

I hear Baggy call out behind me, "I'll bring the Crisco."

Shay responds, "Let's hope it doesn't come to that."

Trying to get rid of that mental image, I race to the bridal suite. What I find there is cringe inducing. Ruthie is flailing around the room with her wedding gown stuck on her head. Syd, Roxy, and Caroline are circled around her, trying to keep her from bumping into things.

Sensing that panic has already ensued, I lift my fingers to my mouth and let out a high-pitched whistle. That makes everyone freeze. Baggy has followed me into the room. She gives me a proud thumbs-up sign because she's the one who taught me how to pierce the silence by whistling like that.

"It's okay," I tell them all, trying to infuse my voice with more confidence than I actually feel. "We'll figure this out."

I approach Ruthie and try to pull the tight gown back up over her head.

"Ow!" she howls. "My hair is tangled in it."

They had already been trying to get it on her by pulling down, but I try that next. It won't budge.

"I think you were supposed to step into it," Baggy says, rather unhelpfully.

Ruthie lets out a frustrated huff of breath. "I tried that. We couldn't get it up."

"On your wedding night?!?" Baggy quips and jabs me with her elbow. No one laughs at her inappropriate joke, so she expands. "They couldn't get it up… get it?"

"We get it, but now is not the time for jokes," Caroline snaps at her mother.

Baggy pokes her lip out in a visible pout. "I was just trying to lighten the mood a little."

Deciding that I'll worry about cheering Baggy up later, I say to Ruthie, "Can you kneel down on your knees…" At Baggy's excited intake of breath, I remind her, "Not now, Baggy," before continuing, "So we can see where your hair is caught?"

When Ruthie maneuvers herself down, there is a collective gasp. Somehow, the front part of her hair has entangled itself around the gown's pearl buttons.

"Mmm, girl, have you ever considered bangs?" Syd asks the bride, which makes the bride gasp before falling over in a faint.

Not wasting any time, Syd jogs to his train case, grabs some scissors and snips Ruthie's hair free of the gown. By the time she comes to, we have the dress off her, and I am working to unwind from the buttons the tangled lock of her hair that has been cut off.

"What happened?" Ruthie sounds woozy.

"Your hair got a major trim," Baggy says, a little too honestly.

Ruthie's eyes widen with alarm. "What? On my wedding day?!?" She reaches up to feel for herself.

"Not to worry," Syd swoops in with a bottle of water. "You drink this, then we'll get you all fixed up."

"My hair," Ruthie says to the room at large as she pulls at her now-short bangs.

Syd stoops down so he can look directly into her face. "Honey, have I ever let you down?" When Ruthie merely stares at him with wide, panicky eyes, he urges her more firmly, "Have I??"

When Ruthie finally shakes her head, Syd says. "That's right… I haven't, and I won't. You will look gorgeous for your walk down the aisle. I promise."

He gets up and flounces towards the dressing room to heat his hair styling implements, but I hear him say under his breath, "Besides, I can't have an ugly bride on my resume. I would never get hired in television again."

We help Ruthie sit up and encourage her to drink the water. I bug my eyes out at Baggy when she says, "Oh-my-go-llygeewillikers," upon seeing Ruthie's jagged, horrendous bangs.

"Her makeup is on point, *isn't it?*" I give Baggy a strong hint not to comment on the impromptu haircut.

Baggy's mouth opens and closes a few times as if she is a fish out of water. I can tell she is dying to say something. To stop her, I assist Ruthie with standing and say, "Let's get you over to Syd, so he can make your hair as beautiful as your face."

The hope-filled gaze Ruthie gives me makes me feel guilty. Syd has already proven himself to be an incredibly talented stylist, but it would take a miracle worker to fix Ruthie's crooked, too-short bangs, which look like they were chopped off by a preschooler.

When I walk Ruthie over to Syd's chair, the tall, lanky man stands between the bride and the mirror, effectively blocking her view of the carnage on top of her head. We get her seated and he leaves the chair facing away from the mirror.

"It must be really bad," Ruthie guesses quietly.

"No," Syd lies convincingly. "I just need a chance to work my magic before the big reveal."

He rubs pomade between his palms and gets to work. Knowing she is in good hands, I head back out to the main bridal suite to figure out how to get the bride into the too-tight gown.

Jamie chooses that moment to crack the door open and peek her head inside. "Everything on track?"

I can't believe she has the audacity to ask this when she knows perfectly well that it isn't. After walking over to block her from fully entering the room, I hiss, "No. The dress doesn't fit, but then you already knew that, didn't you?"

The crestfallen look on the woman's face makes me feel guilty for being so harsh with her. After all, she had tried to warn me. It wasn't her fault the back-up dress I ordered couldn't get here in time.

Jamie's eyes dart to the cameraman standing unobtrusively in the corner, capturing every moment. Evidently deciding he's far enough away, she whispers, "I tried to warn you."

"I know," I admit. "It's just that something seems to go wrong with this wedding at every turn."

"That was the producers' intent, but between the storm and people passing out right and left, they haven't had to implement half of the drama-inducing twists they intended. This wedding is enough of a fiasco without any of our help."

Her almost-giddy tone rubs me the wrong way. I know it's her job to make sure the television show about the wedding is dramatic and riveting, but it's my job to make sure the bride has the wedding of her dreams. It's too bad we can't seem to figure out a way to make both of our goals a reality.

Evidently feeling the same way, Jamie leans in to whisper near my ear. "I hope you've figured out an alternative for the back-up flowers because rumor has it that the ones that wilted on the dock are still better than the big, ugly ones that were just delivered."

"Thank you," I mouth the words at her, truly appreciating the heads-up.

After closing the door behind my friend, who had stuck her neck out for me, even though her loyalties were more aligned with the opposition, I turn and yell, "Baggy, Are you ready for a super-secret, special project?"

*T*he prospect of a top-secret mission makes Baggy's eyes light up like a young child's on Christmas morning. "Will I need a gun?" She's already foraging in her oversized leather Aigner handbag.

"No!" I practically shout, certain that she'll accidentally shoot someone if she whips a gun out of her purse.

The old woman looks disappointed that she won't get to use her weapon, so I stride over to her and lean down to speak close to her face. I infuse my voice with enthusiasm when I ask, "How would you like to go on a mission in search of flowers?"

"Flowers?" Baggy practically spits, obviously disgusted with the idea. "Those aren't dangerous. Send Grandmother Hibiscus out for those. I need to be in on the real action and danger. I'm a spy, you know," she waggles her sparse brows at the last bit, obviously trying to impress me with her unique skills.

I give her a surprised look and make sure my tone sounds uncertain. "Well, if you think Grandmother Rose can handle such an important job, I guess I can ask her." I tap my lip as if I'm deep in thought. Really laying it on thick, I add, "Her last name is Rose, so I guess she might be more qualified than you anyway."

Baggy rears back, angry that I would suggest that Grandmother Rose is more qualified than her. "That prissy old bitty isn't better than me at anything."

Knowing she won't be able to resist the bait, I add, "It's fine if it's too big of a job for you. I'm sure Grandmother Rose will be happy to be in charge of such a vital part of Ruthie's ceremony."

"I'm on it!" She shouts, already heading for the suite's door. "This wedding will have the best, most beautiful flowers you've ever seen."

I can't help smiling at how easily maneuvered the spry old woman is. She's as easy to trick into doing something as a small child. I just hope she doesn't pick all of the resort's lovely flowers. Deciding that they are getting loads of free publicity from having the wedding here, I opt not to worry about it. Besides, their flowers will grow back, right?

Putting Baggy on the flower mission serves two purposes. I have no doubt that she will secure some lovely buds, plus it gets her out of the way in the bridal suite. It would probably only be a matter of minutes before she blurted out to Ruthie that her bangs look ridiculous. We certainly don't need to add a distraught bride to the mix of today's problems.

To myself, I mutter, "She knows not to go outside in the storm to look for the flowers, right?" Deciding that she has enough common sense to have survived this long, I turn to Roxy and Caroline to say, "What are we going to do about this dress?"

The three of us brainstorm, until we deduce that there is only one viable option. Trying to be nonchalant, I go to the styling room to ask Syd if we can borrow his scissors. He gladly hands them to me, but once he has time to process the request, his brow furrows.

I turn quickly and head back into the main suite. He follows close on my heels. "Why do you need them? You're not about to do what I think, are you? Because that would be crazy... That dress is Oscar De la Renta."

His voice trails off to a croaked whisper near the end of the fancy brand name because I am already snipping into the expensive tulle. I focus on my task, careful to cut a straight line. When I look up, Syd has his hand over his heart, gently patting his chest as if I've given him palpitations.

The gasp from the other side of the room comes from Ruthie. She has followed us out here and is looking on in shock as I take scissors to her wedding gown.

"It's going to be fine." I assure her, sounding more confident than I feel. Once I think the cut is deep enough to allow her to step into the dress, I hold a hand out towards the bride.

"Your hair looks gorgeous!" I gush when I

catch my first glimpse of her sweeping, styled bangs.

"You doubted my skills?" Syd narrows his eyes in my direction, but I can tell he isn't truly angry.

Deciding to go the honest route, I say, "Well, yeah. I thought those hacked bangs were beyond hope."

Ruthie's mouth is hanging open as her gaze volleys between us. Finally, she says, "I'm glad I didn't know that."

Roxy comes forward to lead Ruthie over to the gown. The two of us help the bride step into her dress and work together to pull it up. It takes one more snip of the scissors, but soon we have it up and the capped sleeves are on her shoulders.

We stand back to admire our handiwork with twin expressions of concern on our faces. "Umm, does anyone know how to sew?" I ask the obvious question to the room at large.

"I do." A deep voice answers from the crack in the doorway.

I'm surprised when I look up to see Shay peek in. I try but fail to keep the shocked disbelief out of my voice when I ask, "You can sew?"

"You bet," he answers confidently, already strolling into the room. "I've sewn up many a wetsuit tear. A wedding gown can't be that different from neoprene, is it?"

Caroline announces that she has a sewing kit and goes to retrieve it as Roxy and I continue to stare at the back of the gown.

"What are we going to do about this?" Roxy side-whispers to me as she waves a finger over the gape between the buttons and holes along Ruthie's back.

"Not sure," I whisper back, trying to keep from alarming Ruthie.

Proving that we are failing at keeping the problem quiet, Ruthie snaps, "You know I can hear you, right?"

Syd comes around to join us behind her and doesn't even attempt to hide his dismay. "OMGeeee. That doesn't even come close to closing, honey. What did they do––order it two sizes too small?"

"What?!?" Ruthie already knew the dress was too tight, but she isn't aware until that moment how far it is from fastening.

"We'll figure out something," Roxy promises, trying to appease her sister as we all stare at the gaping dress and try to devise a viable solution.

After tapping my index finger against my chin for a long moment, my ah-ha moment arrives. "Rubber bands," I shout a little too loudly, startling the others.

When I get confused looks all around, I clarify. "Pregnant––or otherwise bloated––ladies use them to hold their pants closed when they get too tight to fasten."

Thankfully, no one asks me how I know this. I've never been pregnant, but I have dealt on more than one occasion with serious water retention issues after a night of indulging in too many chips with cheese dip at the Mexican restaurant.

Ruthie turns back and looks at me like I've lost my mind. Her face is scrunched with disbelief when she asks me, "You want me to rubber band my wedding gown together?"

It dawns on me then how tacky that would look. "Maybe we can find some white rubber bands," I suggest lamely.

"I can't believe I'm so fat that we might have to use office supplies to secure my wedding gown," Ruthie practically wails.

We all immediately jump in assuring her that she is not fat.

Shay proves himself to be insightful when he says, "I bet the show's producers ordered the wrong sized dress on purpose. They seem to be willing to do anything to wreak havoc, and therefore surge ratings, on your big day."

"That's exactly what happened," I assure her, even as I look back at the cameraman and wonder how much of this he is catching. Deciding they probably won't air anything that casts them in an unflattering light, I forge on. "They are trying to sabotage every detail of your wedding. That's why I'm here… to keep them from succeeding."

The watery-eyed look Ruthie gives me practically melts my heart. "You're here just because you have my back––even with as horrible as I've been to you lately?"

"Of course," I nod vehemently. "You're my family-by-choice."

We hug, but Syd quickly shuffles us back from each other with a firm warning. "Don't go messing up my masterpiece. You don't want to deal with my wrath."

The idea of sweet, flamboyant Syd's wrath has us all chuckling, which––based on how enthusiastically he joins in––had obviously been his intent. Right in the middle of his guffawing, Syd snaps his fingers and says, "I know how to secure that dress."

When he scurries off to get what he needs, Ruthie quips, "He's not getting white staples is he?"

We all laugh at that––even normally stoic Caroline, who has returned to the room with a small sewing kit.

It's Shay that has us all in stitches, though, when quick as a wink, he responds, "No, that would look silly. I'm sure he's getting some white duct tape."

As we cackle at his silly comment, he holds up his hands and says, "What? I thought duct tape fixes everything."

*S*hay wets the end of the white thread in his mouth and quickly pushes it through the hole in the needle. His nimble fingers work efficiently to patch together the cuts I made in the gown.

Nervous about having him behind her with the sharp needle, Ruthie turns to the side and says, "Don't poke me."

"I won't, but you have to stand still," Shay reminds her.

Syd returns triumphantly to the room, holding a handful of shiny silver ponytail holders in his hand. He joins Shay behind Ruthie and sets about the work of twisting the hairbands to secure her pearl drop buttons.

Caroline, Roxy, and I stand at a loss for how to help as the men work on sewing and tying Ruthie into her dress.

Ruthie grins about the odd situation before saying, "I never dreamed I would have two handsome men securing me into my wedding gown, while the women in my family stand around watching."

We all nod our agreement that this isn't at all how anyone would have predicted things would go.

I see the concerned expression arise on Ruthie's face. "Just one problem, though," she announces. Once she has our undivided attention, she asks, "How is Andrew supposed to get me out of this thing later tonight?"

"I'm sure he'll figure out a way." It's Caroline who makes the suggestive comment, which surprises us all.

Shay keeps his focus on hiding his tiny stitches as he says, "Wild horses couldn't keep me from tearing Lizzie out of her dress, if it was our wedding night."

His marvelous words take everyone by surprise––especially me. I feel my cheeks burning hot, so I turn away and brush at my flour-spotted dress. Biting my lower lip to keep the wide grin at bay, a tantalizing mental image of Shay ripping this dress off me later tonight surfaces in my mind.

An awkward silence ensues after Shay's bold comment. Baggy barges into the room carrying a basket piled high with colorful, wind-whipped, and wet flower buds. I don't have long to worry about if she went out in the storm and picked every flower in the resort because she announces loudly, "The pastor finally arrived, but she has a major case of Montezuma's revenge."

We all stare at her blankly, so she elaborates in

a stage whisper. "That means she has a major case of the shi–," she pauses, remembering her epiphany and amends her last word to "poops."

I hold my hand up to my head, suddenly feeling a massive headache coming on. "Oh no." Ruthie's gaze darts to mine. It's the first time I have shown an outward sign of weakness regarding the non-stop stressors of this wedding. "I was planning to go online to get ordained, so I could act as a back-up for the reverend, but between the storm and everything else," I wave my hands around to the room at large, "I forgot."

I am beginning to feel overwhelmed. Panic makes my stomach churn. I tend to thrive on chaos, but this latest snafu is pushing me over the edge. It's simply too much.

Shay continues his sewing without even looking up as he saves the day again. "I can officiate the ceremony. I got ordained a few months ago to perform an underwater wedding ceremony for one of my buddies."

The immediate relief in Ruthie's gaze is obvious. A deep sigh escapes me as I slowly begin to once more feel in control of the situation. Beaming at Shay, I gush, "You keep saving the day. I could kiss you."

"Maybe later," he teases me, grinning as he continues his stitching.

Just the idea of kissing him––and potentially more––makes heat settle low in my belly. Somehow this lazy slacker keeps coming through with exactly what we need.

Both men stand to their full heights within moments of each other.

"Done." Syd announces before spinning Ruthie in a circle.

I am stunned by how perfectly the back of her dress turned out. It looks like it was made with the shiny silver, crisscrossing ties, and Shay's miniscule stitches are imperceptible––even when I inspect them closely.

"Does it look okay?" Ruthie asks nervously, craning her neck towards the mirror and trying to see their handiwork.

"It looks perfect." Caroline weighs in with her hard-won opinion.

"You look perfect." Roxy tells her sister.

All I can do is nod as the four of us share a watery-eyed hug.

Never one to be left out, Baggy forces her way in and pops up in the middle. "Let's get this party started!"

We all whoop with excitement over the prospect of finally having everything under control enough to actually have this wedding ceremony.

I barely register when Shay asks for and is handed a cell phone. It seems odd that he would suddenly be so interested in a device that he claims to view with such disdain, but I don't pause to question him about it.

After a few quick taps and a gander out the suite's window, Shay announces to the group, "It looks like the eye of the storm is getting ready to pass over us. The wind and rain should calm down for a bit, if you want to try to have the wedding outside."

The delighted expression on Ruthie's face

makes the answer to that question clear. Her voice is filled with renewed hope when she asks, "Really?"

"If we hurry," Shay answers, which makes us all jump into action.

Syd busies himself circling the room and doing final fluff and puffs on each of the ladies, including me. I dive into Baggy's basket of flowers, find the best ones, and tie a ribbon around them to make a bouquet for Ruthie to carry.

"It's lovely." The bride beams at me when I present it to her.

"I picked 'em." Baggy grouches, wanting her share of the credit.

I grin down at the tiny whippersnapper before assuring her, "And you did a marvelous job."

My praise makes the old woman preen with pride. Deciding that this would be a great time to reveal her special job for the ceremony, I lean in and say, "How would you like to be the flower girl for Ruthie's wedding?"

Her blue eyes sparkle at the thought. "Really?" she asks, her face already glowing with anticipation.

I turn to make sure the bribe hasn't angered Ruthie. It is obvious by the loving look she is giving her wacky grandmother that she wouldn't begrudge her this thrill.

When I nod to confirm, Baggy reveals dreamily, "I've always wanted to be a flower girl."

Her face brightens with an idea, and I wonder what the ornery woman is cooking up in her mind. We don't have to wait long to find out because she turns to Ruthie and asks excitedly,

"Can Howie join me? I bet he's never gotten to be a flower girl at a wedding either."

Just as I'm wondering if Ruthie is going to draw the line at having her grandmother's delusional husband act as co-flower girl, the bride's face transforms into a wide smile. "You know, this is my day, so we should be able to break any rules we like. I think you and Howie will make perfect flower girls."

Baggy practically squeals with glee as she darts off to share the news with her husband.

After assessing the weather radar on the phone he borrowed and staring out the window for a long moment, Shay announces to the room, "The eye is almost here. We need to start the ceremony in about fifteen minutes."

The entire room freezes as we all stare at him for a long moment. Ruthie is the one who breaks the silence by saying, "It's go time. Let's do this!"

*O*nce the decision is made to move forward with the ceremony outside, our small group springs into action. We quickly round up everyone and head outside.

It isn't safe to put up the arbor, and it's far too windy for the makeshift aisle to stay in place, but we do our best to make everything else work. Rather than chairs that might topple over and blow away, the guests gather around the beachside location we have chosen, and I direct them on where to stand.

When I notice the contestants from Ruthie's previous reality television show, *Cruising for Love*, standing on the sidelines, I approach them. "No drama, right?"

"Of course not," Cam, the man the producers had selected for Ruthie to marry lifts his shoulders as if the idea that they would cause a problem is preposterous.

I look up at the sky and realize the eye of the

storm is eerily calm when compared with the howling winds and drenching rains we have been enduring. The weather is far from perfect, though, and I wonder how long our reprieve from the battering will last.

Almost as if he can read my mind, Shay announces to the group at large, "We won't have this relatively calm weather for long. The storm's other eyewall is quickly approaching, and when it hits all hell is going to break loose out here."

Once I have the men situated to my satisfaction, I run inside to check on the bridal party. I frantically get them into their spots and signal for the music to start.

Ruthie chooses that moment to pull me in for a hug. "My wedding would have been a complete disaster without you."

Tears are threatening to spill over her eyelids. Syd waggles a finger at us. "I used waterproof mascara, but if you could *not* put it to the test, that would be great."

We grin at each other over his mock outrage, even as a happy tear blazes a trail down my cheek.

"Will you stand up with me as a bridesmaid?" Ruthie asks me.

I look around and realize that everything is under control. This isn't the wedding we would have planned, but it is still somehow perfectly imperfect. After days of running around like a crazy woman on speed, I suddenly don't have anything that needs my immediate attention.

"I would love to be your bridesmaid," I tell her honestly.

With that, it's settled. Baggy hands me some

flowers from her basket that I hold as an impromptu, yet lovely, bouquet as I set off down the aisle.

Roxy follows and takes her place next to me as the Matron of Honor.

Next, Baggy and Howie come down the aisle. Their entrance can best be described as twirly as the two of them dance and saunter down the aisle sending flowers flying into the spiraling wind. Although they are far as can be from a traditional flower girl, they exude carefree happiness and a trail of fragrant blossoms spins in their wake.

On cue, a moving rendition of the bridal march begins, and we all turn to watch Ruthie walk down the aisle arm-in-arm with her proud father. Syd has worked his magic on her makeup and hair, but Ruthie's glow of pure happiness is what truly makes her a beautiful bride.

When she joins Andrew in front of Shay, a single ray of sunshine beams down on them as if they are in exactly the right place in precisely the right moment. The wind swirls Ruthie's long blond hair out around her, making her look ethereal as Shay leads the happy couple in exchanging their vows.

The first hiccup occurs when it is time to exchange the rings. I nearly have a panic attack when everyone looks around in search of the wedding bands. Just as I am berating myself for not effectively handling this detail, Andrew pulls the platinum rings seemingly from mid-air behind Ruthie's ear.

I glare eye darts at him for the ill-advised prank, but Ruthie giggles as if her magic man has just done the most enchanting trick in the world. Deciding it's not my place to berate the groom for scaring me half to death, I plaster on a smile and force my heart rate back down to a normal rhythm.

The remainder of the ceremony goes off without a hitch. I swipe tears from my cheeks as Shay pronounces them husband and wife and gives them permission to kiss.

After a long, passionate kiss, during which Baggy stage whispers to Howie that the newly-weds should get a room, the happy couple turns to beam at the crowd.

Roxy startles us all by bolting past me with her hand raised to cover her mouth. She finds a metal trashcan on the beach and leans over to vomit into it. Kai is by her side in a flash, rubbing a soothing hand over her back.

The momentum of the wedding has been stalled as we all share concerned looks over Roxy's health.

Again, Baggy tries to whisper her words out the side of her mouth to her husband, but she's loud enough for us all to hear. "Do you suppose she's pregnant?"

Grandmother Rose leans forward to say to Baggy, "Just because you can't hear thunder, doesn't mean the rest of us can't, you ridiculous old badger."

Baggy looks furious, but her retort is stalled when Roxy returns. Roxy's cheeks flush red as she assesses the situation and quickly realizes she has just stolen the spotlight from the bride.

"I'm sorry," she says sincerely to her sister. "I

wanted to wait until after your big day to make the announcement."

"Wait… It's true? You're pregnant?" I expect to see fury in Ruthie's eyes over having to share her big moment, but instead she looks utterly thrilled.

At Roxy's confirming nod, Ruthie throws her arms around her sister before announcing to the crowd, "I'm going to be an aunt!"

She gives her sister a long squeeze before turning to pull me into their embrace. "Lizzie, we're going to be aunts!"

I hug them back with all my might, thrilled beyond words to be included. Their forgiveness means everything to me.

We share a long, special moment together, which is only broken when Baggy says, "That baby will only use Baby Bjorn products, right? Because they are the best." She gives an exaggerated wink to the cameraman standing closest to her, which has us all in stitches.

Shaking his head and proving that he has already assimilated into this wild family, Andrew shouts, "Let's go inside before the storm blows us away!"

Our group lets out a collective whoop of excitement before we head inside. Just as the glass door closes behind the last of us, the wind kicks up again and a palm tree crashes to the ground right where we just held the ceremony.

33

*R*uthie and Andrew's reception is a blast. The liquor is flowing freely enough that even Baggy and Grandmother Rose tentatively make up and are slow dancing together on the lobby's makeshift dance floor.

When the cake Baggy and I made is wheeled out and presented to the bride and groom, I snicker quietly as I watch Ruthie gawk at the lopsided concoction. She tries her best to be graceful about it, but it's obvious that she is wondering what kind of loopy pastry chef made it.

Once she and Andrew cut into it and feed each other a bite, she immediately turns to Baggy. "This cake is delicious, like only you could make it. Did you have something to do with it?"

Baggy looks immensely proud of herself. "Maybe," she admits, before adding, "and Lizzie helped."

I nod to confirm before adding, "There was a

slight mishap––involving your real cake, the ground, and Grandmother Rose." I glance over in time to see Grandmother Rose cross her arms and step away from Baggy. Evidently all is not yet forgiven.

"Sorry I missed that," Ruthie quips, before mouthing in my direction the words, "thank you."

When Shay brings me a slice of cake on a gold-rimmed dessert plate, we find a spot to sit down and eat. After watching him take several bites, I say, "Hold on... Are you a cake or frosting man? Because I don't think I can deal with it if you're on the wrong side."

He pauses and looks at my plate where I have been scraping the cake's icing off to eat in sugar-filled mouthfuls. Glancing back at his own plate, which holds an icing carcass where the cake has been carved out of the frosting, he says, "Hmm..."

Swapping our plates, he beams, obviously proud of himself. "We make the perfect team because we each get double servings of what we like."

Unable to argue with that logic, I dive into my second plate of icing as the champagne toasts begin.

Ruthie's co-stars from the previous reality show she was on all give heartfelt-sounding speeches about how happy they are for the newly-weds. I try not to be cynical as I listen to them, but I can't keep the nasty thought at bay that they are each just trying to extend their fifteen minutes of fame.

Thankfully, I'm pulled out of wondering about

that when Jamie runs up to me. I can't get over how lovely she looks after having been 'Syd-ified.' I smile over the word I'm now using in my mind to refer to Syd's miraculous makeovers that he performs with seemingly little effort.

"Guess what?" Jamie's eyes are bright with excitement.

"What?" I infuse my own voice with enthusiasm.

"T.J. just asked me to save a dance for him. Can you believe it? He's never done anything like that before. I didn't even think he realized I am a girl." She's practically giddy.

I smile at her as she twirls around, unable to contain herself any longer. "It's about time he notices what a catch you are."

She gives me a warm hug before darting off to the powder room. I hope the producer doesn't hurt sweet Jamie. Otherwise, he will have to deal with my wrath.

I don't have to stand alone worrying about that for long because Shay sidles up beside me. "Done taking care of everyone else for a few minutes?" He asks me.

It warms my heart that he notices my efforts to make my friends' lives better. When he gently guides me into his arms for a dance, I lean my head on his broad shoulder, enjoying his fresh, outdoorsy scent and the solidness of his firm embrace. It's nice to finally relax for a moment as we sway together to the upbeat ukulele version of *Somewhere Over the Rainbow*.

While we are snuggled together, it dawns on

me that I don't have a place to spend the night. I can't help but wonder if Shay will let me stay with him again. I wouldn't mind the storm sweeping the boat out to sea tonight and causing me to miss my flight home, if it meant time spent in Shay's arms.

Not wanting to be crass, but needing to have this settled, I hint. "It's been too nasty outside to search for your room key."

"I'm sure it's a goner, but not to worry," he assures me. "Maintenance made me a spare."

"Oh," I say flatly, trying but failing, to keep the disappointment out of my tone. When another idea pops into my mind, I say with renewed hope, "Is the power still out in the employee housing, or did they get it restored?"

"They aren't even working on it yet, since the back half of the storm is just now barreling through."

A relieved breath whooshes out of me at this news, but I try not to let it outwardly show. Trying not to sound too forward, I say, "Hmm. Sounds like I'm going to need to find a place to sleep tonight."

Instead of taking my heavy-handed hint, Shay says, "Lucky for you, Ruthie and Andrew will probably be sharing a room tonight. I'm sure she will be happy to let you use the extra one."

I hadn't thought of that, but I wondered if maybe they had already planned for it. "Perhaps, but they might have decreased the reservation, knowing that the two of them would only need one room tonight."

"Maybe," Shay shrugs before adding, "But lots

of people cancelled their reservations, due to the incoming storm. The hotel is no longer anywhere near maximum capacity. I'm sure you can get a real room now."

The disappointment over his rational points nearly overwhelms me. Not wanting him to sense it, I manage to say, "Great," but my heart obviously isn't in it.

At that flat mumbled word, he lowers his chin to look down into my face. He doesn't bother to hide his bemused expression. "Lizzie Lowe, if I didn't know better, I'd think you are disappointed to have your own room tonight."

Taking a deep breath and deciding to be truly bold and daring for the first time in my structured life, I put my heart on the line and say, "I was actually hoping to spend my last night here with you."

Deciding that might not be quite clear enough, since we have already spent the night together, I add, "not sleeping."

Shay's eyes look like they might pop right out of his head over my suggestive declaration. He stares down at me for a long moment. I gaze back up at him without flinching.

When he reaches down and places both of his hands along my jawline, I feel like a cherished, precious jewel. He leans down to gently brush his lips against mine.

I press up into his kiss, immediately craving more, but he pulls back.

His kind eyes are looking down at me with so much affection that his words take a long moment to register in my mind. "You are an amazing woman, but no… I won't spend the night with you."

With those devastating words, he turns and walks away, leaving me utterly stunned and with an aching hole burning in my chest.

34

I stand by myself on the dance floor trying to make sense of what has just happened. My shock turns to horror as I realize that I have just offered my body to a virile, heterosexual male, and he has unequivocally turned me down.

My mouth hangs agape as I look around the room, searching for any sign that can give me answers. Aren't men supposed to always be ready and anxious for sex? I didn't realize that willing, reasonably attractive females were ever given a 'no, thank you' when they were offering a man a night of naked pleasures with no strings attached.

Jamie is the first to notice that something is wrong with me. She scurries over and asks what has happened.

Without thinking I blurt out the problem. "Shay politely declined my offer to spend the night in bed together."

"What??" She asks me with her face scrunched

up in disbelief. It's obvious that she is as perplexed by this turn of events as I am.

I have apparently been too loud with my proclamation because Baggy and Ruthie have now left their dance partners and joined our small circle.

"That can't be right," Ruthie weighs in with her opinion. "Are you sure he understood that sex was on the table?"

"I was pretty clear," I nod, feeling more humiliated by the second.

"What's going on?" Baggy yells far too loudly. "Shay doesn't want to have sex with you? Why the hell––I mean heck––not?" She sounds outraged, but she still looks up towards the ceiling and apologizes for her cursing slip-up.

My mortification over the entire event is multiplying as I realize that more and more people are becoming aware of it from Baggy's loud questioning. Baggy's husband, Howie, and Ruthie's new husband have joined our circle, but even more people are staring.

Baggy's face lights up with an idea right before she suggests, "Maybe he's gay! If so, we should set him up with Syd, that wonderful sweetheart who knows just how to accentuate my natural beauty." She fluffs her silver curls to showcase her point.

"He's not gay." I tell her flatly.

"Too bad," Baggy decides, shaking her head. "He and Syd would make a handsome couple. Wouldn't they?" She looks around at the rest of us to get our opinions.

When Ruthie nods, my irritation with the

entire situation flares. "It doesn't matter because his is NOT gay. He just doesn't want me."

By the end of my statement, I'm practically shouting. Realizing that I'm taking my frustrations out on the wrong people, I place my palm over my mouth and run out of the room, finally allowing the hot tears to flow down my cheeks.

Forgetting the storm for a moment, I run outside and head towards the beach. The strong winds and pounding rain make it difficult to walk. I'm not able to make it far before turning back. Feeling drenched and defeated, I return to the main building seeking solace.

Just inside the door, I lean my head against the wall and slowly slide down to the floor. Wrapping my arms around my knees, I curl into a ball and let the tears flow freely. I sob to release the stress and frustration of the past few days as well as the stinging humiliation of this evening.

It only takes a few moments for Shay to find me. I don't want him to see me like this. My face has to be mussed from the tears mingling with rain creating a smeared mess.

I turn away from him when he stoops down to be on my level. Feeling his warm gaze on me, I mumble, "Go away. I look like a drowned rat."

He chuckles before admitting, "You do look a bit drowned rat-ish, but I'm not going anywhere."

My first instinct is to playfully smack at him for agreeing that I look awful, but I don't want to slip back into our flirtatious banter, since I obviously misread the signs surrounding it. Instead, I swipe the back of my hands under my eyes in a feeble attempt to clean up my face.

Shay's deep voice feels like a soothing balm when he says, "Come on. I got you a room. Let's go get you dried off."

I know that I shouldn't let him carry me, but when he reaches down and scoops me up as if I'm light as a feather, I rest my head on his shoulder and breathe in his heavenly scent.

"You smell like the beach," I murmur.

"Eww... I smell like dead fish, saltwater, and sweat?" He teases as he carries me to the elevator.

"No, it's more like suntan lotion, exotic fruit, and sunshine."

His cheeks puff out with his smile. "Oh, sunshine has a smell, huh?"

"Absolutely," I answer, before adding, "And it's absolutely divine."

When we get on the elevator, he says, "Four," as he bends down so I can reach the button with my finger.

It feels so marvelous being held in his strong arms that I allow myself to forget for a moment that he has shunned my advances. When it comes rushing back, I pull away from his chest to say, "I can stand on my own."

He reluctantly puts me down, and I walk to the far side of the elevator with my arms crossed. Something about this man makes me practically delirious with need, but I refuse to make myself vulnerable again. He has already made it perfectly clear that he isn't interested in me in a romantic capacity. I won't push it because I'm not a glutton for punishment.

The elevator groans to a stop and dings to indicate we have reached the fourth floor. I'm tempted to tell Shay he doesn't need to escort me to my door, but since he has the room key, I step out of the elevator and wait for him, without turning in his direction.

He takes the lead and stops in front of room 410. After reaching into his pocket to retrieve the key card, he pauses to say, "Baggy found me and gave me an earful. For such a tiny thing, she can sure get her point across--even without cuss words."

I notice that he absently rubs his palm over his abdomen. Knowing Baggy, she probably pounded her pointer finger into his stomach to emphasize her message. I can't help but smile as I picture the little old woman giving big, strong Shay a piece of her mind.

"Oh, you find it amusing that she came after me." He grins down at me, obviously absorbing the entire situation in his typical good-natured manner. At my shrug, he turns serious. "She obviously loves you very much. Their entire family does. As they should," he adds, making my eyes dart up to his.

His voice sounds croaky when he asks me, "How could you think that I don't want you?"

"Umm, you made it perfectly clear that you don't." I remind him.

"Does this feel like the heart of a man who doesn't desire you?" He places my palm flat over his chest.

His heart is thrumming rapidly, like it is trying to beat its way right out of his body. I'm confused by the sudden turnaround in his sentiment, but I'm not sure what to ask him. I can't risk inviting him into my room, only to have him deny me again. It would crush my already fragile ego.

"It took every bit of strength I could muster to decline your magnificent offer earlier, and I've been kicking myself for not taking you up on it ever since," he reveals looking down at me so that our faces are mere inches apart.

I want to reach up to kiss him, but I'm too fearful of his reaction. Instead, I lick my lips nervously as I try to work out what to say.

His lids lower as he watches my tongue flick out to wet my lips. "Why do you have to be so damn sexy and irresistible?"

"You don't seem to have any trouble resisting me." I point out.

Proving me wrong, he crushes his lips down to mine. I let out a soft moan as he threads his fingers through the long hair at the nape of my neck. His tongue explores my mouth slowly and thoroughly as if he has all the time in the world, but his hands are greedy as one grips my hip, while the other massages the back of my head.

When he pulls back, I immediately miss his touch. My lips feel swollen and desperate for more of his delicious kisses, but I will not beg.

Swiping his thick hair, which most women would kill for, back away from his face, Shay says, "I don't know if I have the strength to resist you anymore."

My voice sounds husky when I respond, "Then don't."

35

*W*hen he quickly swipes the keycard and opens the door, it dawns on me that this might finally actually be happening. A delicious mix of nerves and anticipation swirl down my spine as I walk into the room and see that my belongings have been brought up here.

"I sweet-talked maintenance into moving your stuff," he reveals, without making me ask.

I can't quite picture Shay flirting with a gruff maintenance man. Perhaps my stereotypical assumption is incorrect and, in actuality, a gorgeous young woman works in the hotel's maintenance department. In either case, I am sure it would be impossible for anyone to resist a full blast of Shay's charm.

Although a one-night stand is completely out of character for me, I am nearly doubt-free about whether or not this should happen. I am confident that if I *don't* spend this night naked in Shay's arms that I will regret it for the rest of my life.

He, however, doesn't seem as sure. As soon as we cross the threshold into the luxurious suite, he paces to the far side of the room. "I should sleep somewhere else."

Moving beyond confusion into frustration, I glare in his direction. "Why?"

"Because I know this isn't what you truly want," he answers, surprising and annoying me.

"How about if you let me decide what I want?" I state it as a question, but we both know it is rhetorical.

Returning my glare, he says, "You might think you want this now, but what happens tomorrow when you go home?" His voice turns softer when he adds, "I know you well enough to realize that having a fling with me would be completely out of character for you. I don't want to do anything that you will feel guilty about later. The last thing I want is to be your one big regret."

"Trust me, my biggest regret has already happened. Ruining Roxy's wedding is something that I will never forgive myself for––even though she and her family have been kind enough to move beyond it."

"It's time for you to let the guilt about that go," he tells me gently. "Besides, Roxy seems pretty damn happy to me. Would she be that giddy with the man she intended to marry?"

There is no question in my mind that Gary could not have possibly been as perfect for her as Kai is, but I can't let myself off the hook that easily. "No, but it wasn't my place to make that decision for her."

"It wasn't," Shay agrees, before adding, "But it

worked out for the best, and it's time for you to let yourself move on."

After nodding to acknowledge that, I decide to bring the conversation back to the topic at hand. Taking a deep breath to summon my daring side, I say, "Look, I've never pictured myself as a quick 'smash and crash' kind of lady, but I don't want to leave this island without getting naked with you."

Shay's eyes widen at my outrageous words, but he says, "You and I making love would be about the furthest thing imaginable from a quick smash and crash."

I smile at the kindhearted, insightful man in front of me. Changing from my rather crass approach, I ask, "Why do you think I would regret a night of bliss spent in the arms of a wonderful, sweet, thoughtful, and sexy man?"

"Who me?" he jokes.

Wanting to erase any doubt left in his mind, I say, "Yes, you. The only thing I'm scared of is walking out of this room tomorrow morning and never feeling the rest of my whole life the way I feel when I'm with you."

Slipping into Baby's famous line from the movie *Dirty Dancing* had been a complete accident, but Shay delights me when he immediately picks up on it. Smiling, he takes long strides to my corner of the room. "Nobody puts Baby in the corner."

With that, I know that he has decided not to fight our mutual desire any longer. When he pulls me into a kiss, I lunge at him, thrilled to finally be taking our relationship to a deeper physical level.

When I reach down to unfasten Shay's pants,

he clamps his hand around my wrist, stopping my progress. I let out a huff of frustration, wondering if he is going to play hard-to-get again. Instead, he kisses the tip of my nose and says, "We have all night. Let's take things slow and savor every moment of our time together."

Loving the sound of that, I force myself to relax and appreciate each touch, tickle, lick, caress, and stroke.

When he releases his hold on my wrist and lightly smooths his fingertips up my arm, a trail of tingling chill bumps arise in his wake. He bends to nuzzle his five o'clock shadow along my neck, so I tip my head to the side to give him better access.

He growls near my ear, "I've wanted to do this since the first moment I saw you."

"Why did you wait so long?" I ask pushing my front into him, loving the zinging electricity created by each spot our bodies connect. I'm delighted to feel his significant erection pressing into my abdomen, obviously craving more.

Moaning as he rubs his hands up to my shoulders and back down to cup my rear end over my dress, he pulls me even tighter to him and says, "I honestly have no idea. If I'd known it would be like this, I would have spent every free moment with you in my arms."

I untuck his shirt and brush my palms up under the fabric, needing to touch his bare skin.

He tips back his head and hisses at the sizzling connection as my hands glide up his back. When he lowers his lips to mine, we meld into each other. Our tongues dance together as our hands explore each other's bodies.

Quickly realizing there are too many clothes between us, we begin peeling away the layers. I turn so he can slowly unzip my dress. Slipping it from my shoulders, I let it pool at my feet and step out of it. It's a sensual move that leaves us both breathing heavy. Soon, we are standing before each other––completely nude and panting with need.

My eyes travel down Shay's naked form. "You're perfect," I whisper, pressing my lips to his chest.

"You're the perfect one," he tells me as he tenderly kisses the top of my head.

We fall into the bed, laughing. It is only after his ministrations have me begging for release that Shay allows his carefully held control to slip. After he slides on a condom and enters me, I cry out in ecstasy over the marvelous, full feeling of finally having him inside me.

Shay proves himself to be a skilled and passionate lover. He uses his fingers, mouth, and manhood to bring me to new heights––multiple times––that I had never before imagined to be possible. We spend the entire night wrapped in each other's arms, rolling around locked in a passionate embrace, resting, and then starting all over again. It is easily the most delightfully sensuous night of my existence.

I don't ever want it to end, but it must.

36

*P*erhaps I'm a coward for sneaking out while Shay is dozing peacefully, adorably snoring with light puffs of air, but I know that I don't have the strength to tell him goodbye. It's tempting to stay here in his arms for a while longer, but that will only make it harder to leave. I have a real life to get back to, with job commitments and a mother who needs me nearby.

By the time I get to the hotel lobby with my luggage in tow, everyone else is there milling about, except for Ruthie and Andrew. The two of them are extending their stay on the island to enjoy some alone time for their honeymoon.

We all ride together in a shuttle to the airport, with the exception of Grandmother Rose, who has arranged for private limo transportation for herself.

Kai keeps a comforting hand at the small of Roxy's back as the rest of us give her tear-filled goodbye hugs near their gate. We get her promise to send us regular pregnancy updates, and we all gladly agree to make a trip to Hawaii as soon as the baby is born.

After leaving them, Baggy announces that she and Howie have been assigned a special super-secret mission in Madrid. Caroline reminds her mother in a stern voice to check in periodically.

"Yes, Ma'am." Baggy gives her daughter a mock salute before grabbing her husband's hand. The two of them run off together like giddy school children.

Jamie shakes her head. "Being outrageous and a little bit crazy must keep you young."

"A *little* bit crazy?" I ask her and the rest of us chuckle.

Once our laughter dies down, I smile sadly at my new friend. I hate it that this is where we part ways––at least for now––but I'm thrilled to see that T.J. is holding her hand. I fervently hope that this isn't the last time I see her.

"Take good care of her," I tell the producer sternly.

"I intend to." He assures me with a toothy white smile, before turning to kiss her cheek. I'm still not at all sure how suitable of a prospect he is for my friend, but he seems to make her happy, so I guess that is what matters.

Jamie blushes a lovely shade of pink when he kisses her, and she beams a radiant smile at me before pulling me into a hug. She whispers near my ear, "Shouldn't you pack Shay into your suit-case and take him with you?"

"I wish," I tell her sadly before adding, "But I

can't see him being content in the landlocked Midwest."

She nods her agreement, but I see the wave of guilt pass over her face. Not wanting to put a damper on her happiness, I whisper to her, "I hope you and the croc live a long and happy life together."

"There's another side to him," she assures me confidently as her cheeks puff out from her wide, knowing smile.

"I'll take your word for it," I tell her, gently squeezing both of her hands within mine. Tired of sad goodbyes, I say, "I'll text you." Then I turn and quickly walk away before the overwhelming sadness of leaving this place and these people can take over.

I sit in the waiting area for our plane next to Roxy and Ruthie's parents. Andrew's quiet, normal family plops down in the row of chairs across from us.

Suddenly, it dawns on me that we are all going our separate ways and returning to our regularly scheduled lives. It's about the last thing in the world that I want to do, even though I know it's what needs to happen.

When the scuffle erupts from the security line, I can't keep the hope at bay that Shay has followed me here and is trying to get to me, like a scene from a cheesy romantic comedy movie.

Disappointment surges through me when I stand to investigate and find that it's just someone angry about having her regular-sized bottle of salon hairspray confiscated.

Shay isn't here, and he isn't coming. He is

probably already back to his 'don't worry, be happy' beach bum lifestyle, without a care in the world. Sigh.

37

There is no denying the immensely relieved look on my boss, Dave's, face when I return to work. "I was afraid you were going to decide you preferred the island lifestyle and not come back to this crazy, hectic office."

I try to muster a smile, but I fear it ends up looking more like a grimace. Going the honest route, I say, "I need to be busy right now."

"Well, that we can handle." He circles his desk after giving me an awkward pat on the back. Once we are seated, he begins rattling off the myriad of decisions, meetings, and speeches that require my assistance.

Having a to-do list a mile long is how I am most comfortable. I make sense out of chaos. That is my one talent. I do my best to embrace my return to the office, but I'm just not feeling it. I go through the motions, but my mind won't focus. My heart longs to be somewhere else, but I firmly refuse to acknowledge that niggling desire.

At the end of the day, Dave stops by my desk. "You seem a little off your game."

I furrow my brow, surprised by the light repri-mand. "Did I mess up something?"

"No, no… nothing like that," he assures me. "You just seem like your mind––or perhaps your heart––is somewhere else today."

"Oh," I nod, surprised by his intuition. "I think I just need the closure of seeing the show tonight to finalize the ending of that tiny portion of my life."

"Makes sense," he nods, then surprises me by adding, "I can hardly wait to see it."

I can't help but grin up at him. "You watch the show? You don't seem like the type to be hooked on reality television."

"Sarah and the girls insist on watching." He tells me before leaning in to say, "They like the way the beach guy gazes at you, like you are the perfect wave. They are rooting for the two of you to get together. Can you give me any insider infor-mation on that?"

I give him a sad look as I splay my hands out to indicate my desk piled high with neat stacks of files and papers. "Spoiler alert… I have crashed back down to reality."

Dave gives me a long, somber look before sitting down with one hip on my desk. We are comfortable with each other, due to long hours spent in the office, but this is the first time he has addressed me more as a friend than an employee. "Let me start off by saying, I hate it when you aren't here."

I smile up at him. Even though I had done as

much prep work as possible for my absence, and left him with back-ups, I'm sure that things fell through the cracks during my time away. There is no denying that I am very good at my job. It's still nice to have the affirmation from my supervisor that I am missed when I'm gone, though.

"But," he says, startling me. I tilt my head to the side and frown up at him, anxious to hear where he is going with this. "I care about you enough as a person to not want work to be your entire life."

"It's not…" I start to argue, but he holds up a palm, effectively stopping me mid-sentence.

"I know how many hours you put in, and I appreciate your extreme dedication."

"It's starting to sound almost like you're firing me." I laugh nervously as I silently pray that isn't the case.

He shakes his head before promising, "I would never do that. In fact, I'll probably be kicking myself as soon as I walk out of here for saying this, but there is more to life than work."

"I know that. I have a great life." I'm starting to feel defensive about how he is attacking my lack of a social circle outside of the office.

Nodding, he says, "I'm sure you do, but as far as I can tell, you don't have a special someone to share it with."

I shrug. It feels strange to be discussing my love life––or more accurately, lack thereof––with my boss.

"As much as I value you as a phenomenal employee, I want you to experience all that life has to offer––even if that means you have to leave. No matter what happens, I only want what is best for you… personally and professionally."

Smiling warily at him, I wonder what he is hinting at. *Is he going to try to force me to date? He can't possibly think he has any right to say anything in that regard, can he?*

Proving that he's not that dense, he says, "I know it's none of my business, but I couldn't help but notice the magnetic attraction between you and Shay."

I'm surprised to hear that he knows Shay's name. Wanting to shut down this line of conversation before it goes into even more dangerous territory, I say, "Shay and I have a definite spark, but he would never be happy here, and I can't move there… End of story."

"Is it?" Dave's kind blue eyes sparkle down at me before he stands and shrugs into his overcoat.

I scrunch my face up in his direction. "Well, yeah."

"Hmm." He responds noncommittally before heading for the elevator and saying, "Have a good evening, Lizzie."

"Thanks," I say almost to myself as I begin packing my own belongings to head home. I'm not sure what Dave's intention was, but the wheels in my brain are now spinning out of control.

38

*R*uthie's parents invite me to watch the wedding show at their house, but I decline their offer. I find that I want to watch it alone in my condo, without the interruptions of other people's comments or the influence of their opinions.

The producers have a tendency to twist things around and creatively cut the footage to make things appear different than they actually are, so I want to view it alone to pair it with my own memories of what happened.

Besides, I remind myself, it's not about me. It's about Ruthie and Andrew's big day. I am just a minor character on the sidelines of their wedding. The world wants to see them get their happily ever after ending. No one cares about what happens to me––except my mom, and apparently, Dave.

Part of me hopes that the show will reveal Shay saying something hateful or flirting with another woman. If I am confronted with evidence that the way he treated me wasn't as special to him as it was to me, it will strengthen my resolve. I need something to latch onto as I struggle to remind myself why I'm not doing everything in my power to be with him.

Just as I'm pulling the piping hot, buttery popcorn out of the microwave, my doorbell rings. I wonder who would be disturbing me right before the show is scheduled to start. Flinging the door open, I try not to acknowledge the surge of disappointment when I see my mother on the other side.

"Hey, Mom!" I purposely infuse my voice with enthusiasm, but it falls flat. Silently, I chastise myself for allowing myself to hope that it might be Shay at my door.

I dump half of the popcorn in a bowl for my mother and join her in front of the television, which is streaming the show from my laptop. We both shovel popcorn into our mouths as we watch the disaster that was Ruthie's wedding unfold on the screen.

When the show takes a commercial break, Mom says, "Phew… It's a good thing I know that sweet girl is married to the man of her dreams because if I didn't have a sneak peek into how it all turns out, I would be sweating." She fans herself dramatically with a butter-stained napkin.

At my nod, she continues, "I bet people are loving this show! Between the storm, the fighting grandmas, and the problems at every turn, it's riveting. I bet the ratings are through the roof."

"You sound like T.J., the executive producer," I tell her.

"It's so good." Mom shovels a handful of popcorn into her mouth before saying around it, "What's up with you and that handsome Shay?"

"Nothing," I lie, shrugging my shoulders.

"Don't lie to your mother," Mom glares at me. "I know you better than anyone in the world." Patting her belly she reminds me, "I carried you right in here for nine tortuous months."

Her eyes dart to the screen. "Oh, shhhh! It's coming back on."

"I wasn't the one talking," I mutter, but she is too engrossed in the show to absorb my words.

The show manages to make me look like the heroine of Ruthie's wedding. I bite my lip as I watch and worry that Ruthie will think I intentionally stole her spotlight again. She handled it okay during the first show because much of it was focused on Baggy's health emergency, but this show was supposed to be about *her* wedding, not me.

As soon as the next break starts, my cell phone rings. When I see Ruthie's number on the screen, I take a deep breath before answering.

I fully expect her to launch into a heated tirade about how I have ruined her big moment, so I am pleasantly surprised when instead, she says, "You have to figure out a way to be with Shay."

"There's nothing to figure out. He lives there, and I live here. It can't work." I remind her.

"Where there's a will, there's a way." She gives me the tired platitude with a smile in her voice.

When I hear Andrew mumbling near her ear, I

say, "Aren't you two supposed to still be honey-mooning it up?"

"Oh, we are," she assures me, making me smile over how giddily happy she sounds. With a sudden intake of breath, she says, "It's coming back on. Thank you for everything you did. I didn't even know about half of it. Gotta go."

With that, she clicks to hang up, and I go back to watching the show with my mom. By the final scene, Mom has tears in her eyes. She turns to me and says, "You are a wonderful friend. You single-handedly saved that wedding."

Uncomfortable with her gushing praise, I say, "I had a lot of help. They just cut it creatively to cast me in a positive light."

Mom frowns at my downplaying of my role. "Why would they do that? They don't bother to make anyone else look good."

I shrug, unsure how to answer.

Taking her time and thinking over her words, Mom says, "Sweetheart, the last thing I want is to encourage you to leave me."

"You sound just like my boss." I tell her, wondering where she is going with this.

After a deep breath, she says, "It's obvious by the way he acts, and the way he gazes at you when he thinks you aren't looking, that Shay is falling in love with you."

"No," I shake my head, trying to let her know that she's crazy.

"He is." She uses her firm tone with me, which effectively shuts down any further back-talk from me. Softening her expression she asks, "Do you have feelings for him?"

Feeling the tears pooling in my lower lids, I simply nod. Making a valiant attempt not to let them fall, I say, "I do, but we aren't right for each other."

"Because of the distance?"

My confirming nod allows a few of the welling tears to escape and blaze trails down my cheeks. Mom immediately comes over to put a comforting arm around me.

"If you want to make it work, you'll figure out a way. Lots of couples do."

I swipe my hand at the free-flowing tears before revealing, "It's not just that."

"Tell me," she encourages before waiting silently for my response.

"He's a slacker, who is content to sit on the beach all day and call it work. I'm a workaholic, who doesn't know how to relax––even on an island vacation." The volume of my voice is practically at a yell by the time I reach the end.

Mom taps her chin with her finger before saying, "I'm pretty sure I've heard an old motto about opposites attracting."

I give her a wobbly smile over her lame attempt at humor before saying sadly, "Attraction isn't our problem. Moving beyond anything more than a smoking-hot physical relationship that has no potential of a future is our roadblock."

"I'll pretend I didn't hear the 'smoking-hot physical' part because... Eww."

I can't help but snort out a laugh at her over-the-top, appalled reaction to my revelation that Shay and I are hot for each other.

Turning serious, Mom says, "I'm just kidding,

of course. I want you to find the love of your life, and if that person happens to make you want to live on an exotic tropical island, then I'll happily come visit. I need to make time for more vacations anyway. My body could use the extra Vitamin D from all of that sunshine."

"I don't want to move away from you, or my job." I tell her, even as my brain churns with a potentially exciting idea.

"You can't get away from me." She smiles, before adding, "Maybe I could have a guest room at your place, so I can come visit whenever I have time. Think of the frequent-flier miles I could rack up!"

I appreciate how supportive she is being, but I'm still not sure. "I don't want to upend my life for a boy."

"If he's the right boy, then you'll always regret not trying."

Her sage advice strikes a chord with me. Nodding, I decide, "I need to see if it's real," I run to my bedroom to toss some hot-weather clothes into my suitcase.

Mom yells out that a car is on its way to give me a ride to the airport even as she jumps onto my computer to book my flight.

I'll call Dave on the way to the airport to arrange for more days off. It shouldn't be a problem since he already practically gave me permission to quit and follow my heart.

After I give my mom a goodbye hug, I fling open the door and nearly fall into Shay, who is just raising his fist to knock.

39

"Oh!" I stop short, startled to see the man I was going to see standing on the other side of my threshold.

"Hi!" Shay breaks into a wide smile, obviously thrilled to see me.

I beam back at him. "I was just coming to see you."

"Guess I beat you to it," he says good-naturedly.

I frown as I look behind him and see a camera crew. T.J. and Jamie are standing just behind them. "I thought you guys were headed back to California."

"We circled back and never left the island," Jamie tells me. "Once I saw the footage for the show, I had the feeling there would be a great opportunity for some follow-up shots between you and Shay."

T.J. smiles down at her before bending down to give her a light kiss. "And you were right."

While the two of them grin like fools at each other, it dawns on me that this reunion might not be what I initially thought. Turning to Shay, I say, "So, they encouraged you to come here."

"What?" He sounds stunned. "No! This was all my idea. They just insisted on following along."

My mother chooses that moment to insert herself into the conversation. "Shay? I'm Lizzie's mom, Layna."

Shay extends a polite hand in her direction. "It's wonderful to meet you."

Ignoring his offered hand, Mom pulls the surprised man in for a hug. "I feel like I know you already from the show."

Quickly reacting to the situation, Shay hugs her back. I hear him say, "I feel like I know you because I adore your daughter more than words can say."

The look my mom gives me over Shay's shoulder before she releases her tight hold on him speaks volumes. If she had any uncertainty lingering about him, he has just cleared it away.

When the two finally separate, Shay asks me, "Why were you coming to see me?"

I glance towards the camera, suddenly feeling slightly self-conscious. When I turn back to Shay and see his loving gaze, a newfound, bold confidence overtakes me. "I was coming to tell you we should be together."

Shay's ocean-blue eyes practically dance at this revelation before he pulls me into his arms. "I couldn't agree more."

He tilts his head down and brushes his lips against mine. He cups the sides of my face between his palms as if I am the most precious treasure in the world. The electricity zings delightfully between us as we forget everyone else is there and simply enjoy our reunion.

Pulling back, Shay takes in his surroundings for the first time and asks, "Is this place big enough for two, or will we need to move to a larger apartment?"

I don't even bother to hide my stunned expression. "You are going to move here? You'll be miserable. Have you ever even seen snow?"

He chuckles at my last question before assuring me, "I'm sure I can handle it. It's worth it to be where you are, and I could never be miserable with you by my side."

He answers my questions out of order, but I'm overjoyed by his responses. I can't believe he is willing to give up his relaxing island lifestyle for me.

It dawns on me then that Shay's job skills don't translate at all to life in the Midwest. My brow must be furrowed because Shay rubs his hands lightly along my forearms and asks, "What is it? Are you not sure about us?"

For the first time since I've met him, the handsome man before me looks worried. I quickly appease his concern. "No, it's not that. I'm sure about us."

His expression immediately shows relief, even as he prompts me with, "But? ..."

"But, I can't imagine what you'll do for a job, if you live here. We don't have a big watersports industry."

His chuckle startles me. "You really think that all I can do is hang loose on the beach?"

He doesn't sound offended, but I'm beginning to sense that I might have underestimated him. Since he seems to be awaiting an answer, I say, "No…" but it comes out more like a question than an answer.

"I built the beach hut into a thriving business. I should be able to sell it for a tidy profit, so I can use that money to fund a venture here." Putting his hand on his chin as he thinks about it, he says, "Maybe I'll look into opening a skateboarding park or a state-of-the-art arcade."

His statements shock me. I stand there blinking at him with my mouth agape for a long moment. When I finally regain my wits enough to clamp my mouth shut, I remain at a loss for words.

Evidently sensing that I am too stunned to speak, Shay goes on. "I'm not meant to live my life in a cubicle. I've known that since I was young. So, I used my MBA to create a business where I actually enjoy what I'm doing. I look forward to going into work every day. I'll just need to create something similar here… with you."

My mind is swirling with his marvelous reve-lations… *Shay has his MBA, and he's a successful business owner?* Blurting out the first thing that pops into my head, I say, "You're not a slacker."

He gives me a good-natured smile, "No, not even a little bit. But it's thrilling that you fell for me, even when you thought I had no ambition. You must reallllly like me."

"I do." I purr up at him before amending it to, "Actually, I think I love you."

"You think?" Shay pretends to be offended. "Well, you better catch up quick because I know I love you."

We seal our proclamations with a long kiss, managing to forget the others in the room until T.J. says, "This is fantastic footage. The viewers are going to eat it up. Do you two want to go by the hashtag Shay-zie or Liz-ay on social media?"

Reluctantly stopping our glorious kissing, we turn to look at the producer. He appears to be completely serious as if this is the most important thing in the world for us to focus on in this moment.

When I burst out with laughter, the others follow suit, with the exception of T.J. and the stoic cameramen.

Turning to face Jamie, T.J. sounds perturbed when he asks, "What's so funny? I don't get it."

His annoyed questions only make us laugh harder. Jamie's expression softens when she looks up at the producer whom she adores. "I think they're fine with letting you choose," she tells him.

We both nod our agreement with her statement.

Looking up into Shay's eyes, I say, "I just have one minor modification to your marvelous plan."

"Anything," he offers freely, gazing right back down at me.

Letting go of my cautious fears and constant need to do what is expected, I say, "Instead of you moving here, I want to move to Antigua with you."

There is no denying the thrilled expression on

Shay's face as his eyes crinkle adorably at the sides. "Are you sure?"

Nodding and smiling, I tell him honestly, "I've never been so sure of anything in my entire life."

With a whoop of excitement nearly loud enough to be heard all the way to Shay's island beach hut, he picks me up and twirls me around. We are so caught up with each other that I barely register when the show crew and my mother slip quietly out the front door of my condo.

After many celebratory kisses Shay pulls back to look at me. A tiny worry line appears between his dark eyebrows. I run the tip of my finger along it and ask, "What's wrong?"

"What about your job? Won't you miss your mother? Will you be able to handle living so far away from everyone?" The questions come out in a rush, and I am touched that he is so concerned about my emotional wellbeing.

Suddenly, our roles are reversed, and I am the one calming Shay's frazzled nerves. With a confident smile, I tell him, "Don't worry, I have a plan."

The worry line on his face immediately disappears. "I should have known you would have it all worked out in your brilliantly organized mind."

Nodding, I jump into his welcoming arms, and let him carry me into our happily ever after.

EPILOGUE

I pace across the same bridal suite we used to get ready for Ruthie's wedding. "What was I thinking, letting them film our wedding?"

"It will be fine," Ruthie assures me as she fluffs the ribbons on my bouquet of daisies surrounding a single bright hibiscus.

"Don't worry," Jamie assures me. "I made T.J. promise not to pull any stunts." She looks confident in the knowledge that he will abide by her request. I hope she's right.

My nerves are jittery, not because I have any doubts that I'm marrying the right man, but because of the monumental meaning of this day and the vows I'm getting ready to make. It all feels overwhelming as my stomach roils and threatens to revolt.

"I wish Roxy was here." It's at least the thousandth time I have thought it, but the first time I have voiced it aloud.

"She is!" Jamie proclaims with obvious pride as she presents me with an iPad.

I feel confused because I know Roxy just had her baby and isn't able to travel. When I glance at the tablet's screen, I am thrilled to see the face of my exhausted-looking, but obviously happy, life-long best friend.

"Hi!" I smile at her, thrilled to have this live connection with her across the miles.

Her eyes immediately fill with tears. I'm not sure if they are a result of her postpartum hormones or due to seeing me in all my bridal glory until she says, "You are such a beautiful bride!"

"Thank you." I tell her, feeling immensely grateful for her presence.

"No tears!" Syd shouts from across the room, effectively letting me know not to muss his marvelous makeup job. Despite the conniption fit he had when he saw the plain white sundress I am choosing to wear as my wedding gown and the white linen button-up shirt Shay is opting for, even the stylist now agrees that the understated and casual selections are perfect for us.

I nod to acknowledge his request and take a deep, calming breath.

Turning back to Roxy on the screen, I say, "Let me see that handsome young man."

She tilts her own device down, so I can look at the perfect baby boy cradled in her arms. We all squeal and fawn appropriately over how gorgeous he is.

When Roxy's face reappears on the screen, I turn serious and say, "I always thought you would be standing right beside me when I got married."

"I will be!" Roxy exclaims, confusing me.

For a moment, I wonder if she has taken the risk of travelling with her newborn baby. She assuages that worry by saying, "Ruthie is going to carry the iPad down the aisle with her, so we can both be your Matrons of Honor!"

"Perfect!" I say as I clap my hands together excitedly.

Jamie interrupts us when she taps her clipboard and says, "It's time to head downstairs."

I can't help but smile at her as I say, "It's so strange to have someone else planning my wedding, when I've turned planning destination weddings into my career."

"I just hope I can live up to your high standards," Jamie says.

"Everything is wonderful," I assure her, but my gaze is drawn by Baggy, who is standing just behind Jamie, waving her hand in a continuing circular motion.

It takes me a moment to understand what the woman wants from me, but when it dawns on me, I give her a knowing smile. Turning to look directly at the camera for the first time all day, I say in a loud and clear voice, "I couldn't have planned a better wedding myself... as the proprietor of Island Hopping Dream Weddings."

"That's my girl!" Baggy pumps her fist, obviously wholeheartedly approving of me shamelessly plugging my new, but already-thriving, destination wedding planning business to the camera.

Mom gives me a watery-eyed, proud look before pulling me into a warm hug. "I'm so happy for you, sweetheart." Evidently deciding not to be at all subtle, she adds, "I think I could be quite content living in a one-person thatched roof hut by the ocean––especially if I have grandbabies to look after."

I can't help but chuckle at her pushy hint. Shaking my head, I say, "And so it begins…"

After we share happy looks all around the room, I am quickly rushed downstairs. The ceremony where Shay and I vow to share the rest of our lives together goes by in a delightful blur. I can't remember the specifics––other than it races by faster than I could have imagined and makes me happier than I would have dared to dream. At least the video footage from the show will give me a wonderful reminder of this glorious day.

After a traditional island dinner that I'm sure is delicious, but I barely taste, my husband and I sway slowly together on the dance area, which has been cordoned off in the sand on the beach. Looking up at him and thinking that I can't possibly get any happier, I say, "You know, my mother has already started hinting that she's ready for grandchildren."

Shay's eyes widen with surprise as he stares down at me. "Are you open to that, or do you want to just enjoy being married for a while first, Mrs. Sanders?"

I enjoy the sound of my new last name, especially coming from my husband's lips. Taking a moment to really ponder for the first time the idea of becoming a mom, I say, "Hmm…"

Shay focuses solely on me, awaiting my verdict.

"I plan on enjoying every moment being married to you. Plus, I think having a child will only enrich our lives further. Besides, it will sure be fun trying to get pregnant."

His wide-eyed stare makes me wonder if I'm rushing to the next step too fast, so I quickly add, "But only if you're ready."

Rather than answering me, he takes my hand within his own much larger one and we jog together towards our tiny seaside cottage. The laughter of the gathered guests sails on the wind out over the ocean as they all realize why we have so quickly bolted away.

I don't have a care in the world, other than living in the moment with the love of my life.

———

Do you want to read the rest of the books in The Escape Series? Let your mind be whisked away to where the palm trees sway with *Aloha, Baby!*, *Getting Lei'd*, and *Cruising for Love*.

If you've already read the entire Escape Series, enjoy another fun beach read series when you peek inside Fern's diary. The Keys to my Diary: Fern (Book 1) is FREE at most major e-book retailers!

THE ESCAPE SERIES BOOKS

Aloha, Baby! ~ A prequel novella

Ready to escape to Hawaii? Let this novella whisk your mind away to where the palm trees sway!

Alone and pregnant... Leilani Kehele never thought those words would describe her, yet that is exactly how she finds herself in *Aloha, Baby!*

Feeling like a huge disappointment to her

family, Lani turns to her two handsome and loyal best friends, Kai and Honi, for advice.

In an attempt to arrange the best possible outcome for this challenging situation, the three hatch a plan to give Lani's baby a father. Will it work? Will Lani and her baby discover their happily-ever-after ending?

Escape into the enchanting Hawaiian Islands now with Leilani, Kai, and Honi while you read this heartwarming tale of friendship, love, and triumph after heartbreak.

Visit annomasta.com for details.

Getting Lei'd

Jilted by text message. Honeymooning with her grandma. The resort's bartender may look like Jason Momoa, but Roxy is NOT interested.

Being jilted almost-at-the-altar by text message is not at all how prim and proper Roxy Rose thought her wedding day would go.

Getting dragged on her Hawaiian honeymoon by her excessively self-centered sister and outlandishly irreverent grandma is the icing on the horrible wedding day cake.

Can Kai, the resort's hunky and talented chauffeur/bartender/flame-thrower, turn this disaster of a trip into a romantic adventure to last a lifetime?

Or will his mysterious secrets keep their love from blossoming?

Escape with Roxy into the enchanting Hawaiian Islands as she finally discovers the joys of hanging loose and "*Getting Lei'd.*"

Available on at most major ebook retailers.

Cruising for Love

A reality TV show looking for ratings. Kim Kardashian wannabes on a cruise ship. What could possibly go wrong?

Get swept away with Ruthie Rose as she searches for true love on the reality show, *Cruising for Love*!

It is a dream come true for effervescent Ruthie when she is selected to star on a hot new reality television show.

Without bothering to read the pesky contract, Ruthie signs on the dotted line and sets sail on her high-seas adventure.

Join Ruthie as she navigates the many twists, turns, and crushing tidal waves of drama the producers have in store for her on the not-so-real, reality show, *Cruising for Love*.

Sail away with *Cruising for Love* because you deserve an escape to the islands in Ruthie's exciting adventure!

Available at most major ebook retailers.

REVIEWS: BEST. GIFT. EVER.

Now is the time to help other readers. Many people rely on reviews to make the decision about whether or not to buy a book. You can help them make that decision by leaving your thoughts on what you found enjoyable about this book.

If you liked this book, please consider leaving a positive review. Even if it's just a few words, your input makes a difference and will be received with much gratitude.

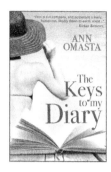

Hi, there! Would YOU like to take a peek in my diary?

Wait, we haven't been introduced. My name is Fern, and by some wonderful stroke of good luck, I live in the beautiful, tropical Florida Keys.

My life is wacky, often wild, and always entertaining. From my love-hate relationship with the book, *The Secret*, to my encounters with cursing parrots and skittering crabs, the summations of my offbeat life will make you laugh right along with me.

It is a particularly exciting year because I finally meet the man of my dreams! Or is he?

This fast-paced story is an intimate look inside my life as I go all-in and hand over the keys to my diary. Go ahead...Take a PEEK!

Spend some time with the lady Kirkus Reviews calls 'fun, likable company.' Get your copy of *The Keys to My Diary ~ Fern* today.

P.S. Now featuring a BONUS epilogue!

>> FREE Download at most major ebook retailers.

ABOUT THE AUTHOR: ANN OMASTA

Ann Omasta is a USA Today bestselling author.

Ann's Top Ten list of likes, dislikes, and oddities:

1. I despise whipped cream. There, I admitted it in writing. Let the ridiculing begin.
2. Even though I have lived as far south as Key Largo, Florida, and as far north as Maine, I landed in the middle.
3. If I don't make a conscious effort not to, I will drink nothing but tea morning, noon, and night. Hot tea, sweet tea, green tea--I love it all.
4. There doesn't seem to be much in life that is better than coming home to a couple of big dogs who are overjoyed to see me. My other family members usually show significantly less enthusiasm about my return.

5. Singing in my bestest, loudest voice does not make my family put on their happy faces. This includes the big, loving dogs referenced above.

6. Yes, I am aware that bestest is not a word.

7. Dorothy was right. There's no place like home.

8. All of the numerous bottles in my shower must be lined up with their labels facing out. It makes me feel a little like Julia Roberts' mean husband from the movie *Sleeping with the Enemy*, but I can't seem to control this particular quirk.

9. I love, love, love finding a great bargain!

10. Did I mention that I hate whipped cream? It makes my stomach churn to look at it, touch it, smell it, or even think about it. Great––now I'm thinking about it. Ick!

** I would LOVE to send you a free copy of my novella, Aloha, Baby! Visit annomasta.com for details. **

LET'S STAY IN TOUCH!

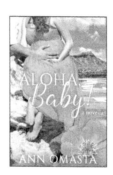

Escape into the enchanting Hawaiian Islands by reading this heartwarming tale of friendship, love, and triumph after heartbreak.

Free when you join the author's VIP reader group. Tell us where to send your free novella.

Visit annomasta.com to get it.

COPYRIGHT

A HUGE thank you to:
  - Marianne Nowicki (Cover artist)

- Dana Lee, Lee Clarity Consulting (Editing/Proofreading)

- The wonderful members of Ann's Clan and Ann Omasta's Reader Group. I wouldn't be able to do what I love without you!

.

Printed in Great Britain
by Amazon